I0682049

The Teaching

Part 1:

The Unleashing

by

Derrick High

IEM TEXAS

Island Entertainment Media

ATTENTION: ORGANIZATIONS AND CORPORATIONS

Island Entertainment Media Books may be purchased for
educational, business, or sales promotional use. For information,
please e-mail the Special Markets Dept. at

IEM Texas

1001 N. Travis
Sherman, TX 75090

Copyright © 2015 by Island Entertainment Media

ISBN-13: 978-0692515266 (Island Entertainment Media)

ISBN-10: 0692515267

Edited by Paula Howell

Printed in the United States of America

Visit Island Entertainment Media on the World Wide Web at www.iemTexas.com

Produced, Distributed, & Published by:

www.IslandEntertainmentMedia.com

I would like to dedicate this book to my mother, Carolyn High.

Table of Contents

Chapter One

"Wake up, Jonathan! Wake up and get ready for breakfast," his mother, yelled.

Jonathan Bailey rolled over, looked at the clock and realized it was 6:30 am. He lay there deep in thought. This was his last year of high school, and he planned to enjoy it. Suddenly, the door to his room opened and his little sister Caroline came bursting in. She jumped on his bed and began dancing around him in her red and black pajamas. She laughed and kept hollering for him to wake up and finally flopped onto his back. Almost out of breath, Jonathan gently rolled her off onto the bed, jumped up and ran into the bathroom.

Caroline, his only sibling, was 8 years old and the two of them thought the world of each other. He did a great job of helping their mother raise them after their father died during a traffic stop a year after Caroline was born.

Caroline had followed Jonathan and was beating on the bathroom door yelling,

"Mom said to get ready for school. And you promised you'd cook me breakfast."

"Come downstairs and leave your brother alone," said Mrs. Bailey. Grabbing Caroline's hand, she led her daughter out of the room. Turning back she said, "Jonathan, you need to hurry. I have a surprise waiting for you downstairs. Somebody's waiting to see you."

Knowing how persistent his little sister was, he cautiously peeked around the door. Just as he expected, Caroline was waiting. She grabbed his shirt, and pulling him out of the bathroom, she began wrestling with him. Jonathan let himself fall to the floor and they both laughed. As she lightly punched him, Caroline reprimanded him, "You promised you would cook me breakfast and you lied."

"Caroline, "their mother called from downstairs, "Come down here and leave your brother alone so he can get ready! And you'd better not tell him who's waiting downstairs." Jonathan picked Caroline up, playfully threw her on the bed and began tickling her. He kept asking who was downstairs, but all she could do was laugh. Between giggles, Caroline managed to yell, "Mom, help me! Come and get Jonathan before I tell him." Little did the kids know, Mrs. Bailey was already standing in the door way.

"Jonathan, you need to hurry up and get dressed. We'll go downstairs and you lock your door. You know how your sister is." Jonathan did just that. He walked over, sat on the bed and slowly laid back. With his eyes closed, he laid there for a minute when suddenly a man appeared to him as in a vision. He was a tall Caucasian man, bald and wearing a white robe with a gold belt.

"It's time to face your destiny, and we don't have a lot of time," Jonathan heard the man say. Startled, Jonathan sat straight up, trying to figure out what had just happened. Was it real? Before he could give it too much thought he realized his mother was calling him.

"Are you dressed yet? Someone down here is getting very impatient with you."

Forgetting about the man in the white robe, Jonathan started to get ready for the day. His thoughts quickly went back to the visitor waiting for him downstairs. Standing at the mirror in the bathroom, he heard that voice again.

"Jonathan, it's time."

"Time for what?" Jonathan asked, as he looked around to see where the voice came from. Suddenly Mrs. Bailey was knocking on the door.

"Jonathan, hurry up," she scolded. He got in the shower and began washing his face when he realized the water was scalding hot, but oddly enough, it was not burning him. He knew how hot the water could get; remembering the time Caroline got her feet burned. He quickly finished and got out of the shower, his thoughts still scattered. With Mrs. Bailey still rushing him from downstairs, he rushed to get dressed and almost put his pants on backwards. Finally, regaining his composure, he dressed, grabbed his comb and ran downstairs. His face lit up at the sight of his uncle Philip standing in the living room.

Philip stood 6'2" and was a stout man. With dark hair and blue eyes, he was one of the world's most eligible bachelors. Being the owner of three of the world's largest uranium refineries, Philip was very wealthy and powerful. He also worked closely with the government. His busy schedule kept him from seeing the family as often as he would like, but whenever he could, he stopped in to check on his brother's widow and children.

Philip was already holding Caroline in his arms when Jonathan entered the room. As he put her down, Philip asked,

"Johnny Boy, how are you doing?" Jonathan loved his uncle, but seeing him made Jonathan miss his Dad even more

since they looked so much alike. Giving him a big hug
Jonathan asked, "How's it going, Uncle Philip?" They stood
there for a minute or two smiling and Philip just looked at his
nephew. Jonathan wondered what he was looking at, but before
he could speak, Caroline became impatient and begged him,

"Jonathan, go outside!" She couldn't say anymore as her
mother quickly covered her mouth. Mrs. Bailey couldn't keep
the smile from her own face. Noticing the smile, Jonathan
asked, "What's going on Mom, Uncle Philip?"

"Go outside, Son," Philip told his nephew as he headed
towards the door. Having a younger sister who loves to cry
wolf, Jonathan was leery, but slowly opened the door to peek.
Philip winked at Mrs. Bailey. Caroline, who could not wait any
longer, ran to open the door and hit her brother in the head.
"Ouch!" Jonathan cried. He looked at Caroline, shook his head,
picked her up and went outside. He never dreamed he would
see a brand new black convertible Ferrari sitting in their
driveway. He ran around the car and put Caroline in the
passenger seat and he climbed in behind the wheel and turned
the radio on.

"That was a very nice thing to do for Jonathan,"
Katherine Bailey told Philip. He replied, "That's not all, Kate.
I have another surprise for him." He continued, "I'm as proud
of our valedictorian as you are. You have done an excellent job

with the kids. Now when are we going to find you a date, friend or something?"

"I'm not looking for a friend or date," she replied. "I'm doing fine with just my children. And besides, we're great by ourselves."

They both turned their attention back to the kids who were having fun singing to the radio.

"Where will you stay?" Katherine asked Philip. "Don't worry about me, Kate.

You know I'll be fine. Besides I always have a lot of late night meetings."

Jonathan got out of the car and hugged his uncle again.

"Thank you Uncle Philip for what you've done."

"That's not all," Philip replied with a grin. He took his wallet from his back pocket and removed a debit card. "This is for you," he said, handing it to Jonathan.

"Don't spend it all in one place."

Hearing the amount on the card, Katherine quickly grabbed it away from her son. The two men just stared as she danced around with the card. Realizing how silly she must look, she stopped and stood there, embarrassed, her hair disheveled. She was more excited than Jonathan was.

"Mom, what are you doing?" he asked her.

"Nothing," she replied, removing the hair from her face. Jonathan already knew his mother would keep the card, as did Philip. With a quick glance at each other, the two men grabbed for the card at the same time. Being a step ahead of them, Katherine jerked the card back and caused them both to miss. "I'm keeping this, you're only eighteen and have no need to carry this much money on you," she told her son. Everyone knew there was no point arguing with her, so Jonathan and Philip shrugged their shoulders at each other and smiled.

"Well, it's time I was heading out of here," Philip said as he picked Caroline up. As he bent down, Jonathan noticed the necklace around his uncle's neck. It was black marble with a black diamond in the center.

"Cool necklace, Uncle Philip," Jonathan remarked.

"Thanks," Philip replied. "I got it on a trip to China."

Katherine took Caroline out of Philip's arms and led her into the house.

"We have to get you ready for school," she told her.

"You know, you're never going to get that card away from her," Philip told Jonathan, nodding towards Katherine.

"I know," his nephew replied. Chuckling, he added, "You know how she is.

She'll probably redecorate the house with it, go shopping, or take a vacation…." They walked towards Philip's truck. "How long will you be in town, Uncle Philip?"

"We just got a new contract so I should be around for a while. We'll get together while I'm here, I promise," he said. "And next time I'll stay longer."

"Great!" Jonathan exclaimed as he hugged his uncle. "That would be great."

Philip slid into the driver's seat and rolled down the window.

"You take care of your mother and sister. Keep those grades up. Oh, and good luck trying to get that card away from Kate."

 Philip chuckled.

Jonathan stood and watched as Philip drove off. His uncle was proud of him, and that made him feel proud of himself; prouder than he had felt in a long time.

Hearing something behind him, Jonathan turned to find the radio still on in his car. He slid behind the wheel and just sat there. He loved his new car. Now he wouldn't be just another nerd who got good grades. Charles was going to love the Ferrari. Jonathan didn't have many friends, but he did have Charles Bradley. Charles was rich and spoiled. He got everything he wanted as soon as he wanted it. His parents were always out of town so Charles did whatever he wanted. Jonathan was lucky to have him, especially since Charles always kept his friend out of trouble. People often picked on Jonathan. Not only was he smart, but he was also small.

Poking her head through the open window, Katherine reminded her son, "You know, you still have to go to school today. Jonathan turned off the radio and hurried into the house.

"I'm glad Uncle Philip came to see us, and not just because of the car," Jonathan said to his mom. "He's going to be in town awhile, so we should get to see him more."

Katherine nodded, finished brushing Caroline's hair and they headed out the door.

"Don't be late for school," she chided her son one last time.

"I know, I know," he answered. He went back upstairs to finish getting ready.

"Get ready." The voice was quiet, but audible. Jonathan turned around but nobody was there. Checking the clock, he realized he didn't have time to worry about strange voices. His biggest worry was not to be late for school.

Chapter Two

Jonathan had the biggest smile on his face as he pulled the Ferrari into the school parking lot. Opening the door to get out, he suddenly heard a phone ringing. It was coming from somewhere in his car. After looking under the seats, he realized it was in the glove compartment. It was still ringing as he retrieved it, so he answered it, "Hello?"

It was Uncle Philip.

"I forgot to mention your last gift," he said.

"Awesome," Jonathan replied.

"Now we don't have an excuse to not keep in touch."

"Absolutely!"

"Call me if you need anything."

"Thanks, Uncle Philip." Jonathan turned the phone on silent, put it in his pocket and sat there watching students walk past. Krista Golden. He didn't blink. He had been fond of her forever and a day. They had known each other ever since the first grade. Like Jonathan, Krista was smart. She was also on the cheerleading squad. He adored her, but she had a boyfriend. Standing 5'8" tall, she was skinny, with brunette hair and a killer smile. Krista looked at Jonathan but before he could smile at her, Michael, her boyfriend, blocked his view. Michael was a bully, always had been, even before Krista came along. The bullying got worse once Michael and Krista started dating. He was 6'2" and nothing but muscle. He was the captain of the baseball team and hated Jonathan with a passion.

Jonathan's mind went back to last year's homecoming game. He and Krista were talking behind the bleachers when Michael and a few of his friends ambushed him. Jonathan blacked out and when he came to, he found himself standing in the rain while everyone, including Michael was getting off the ground. The two enemies stared at each other momentarily and Michael started walking towards Jonathan. Just in time, there came Charles. Bradley to the rescue again. Michael took Krista's hand and they scurried away.

"Loving the car," Charles said, bringing Jonathan back to the present. He climbed into the passenger seat. "Two thumbs up," he told his friend. "Now tell me who you stole it from."

"It's all mine," Jonathan beamed. "A gift from my uncle." Jonathan showed off the cell phone.

"I'll say," said Charles.

"I'm moving up," Jonathan replied.

"You're going to have to start standing up to Michael, you know," Charles said.

"I can't protect you forever."

They got out of the car and headed for the courtyard when Jonathan locked eyes with a girl he had never seen before.

"Who's that?" Charles asked.

"Must be new, I've never seen her before."

"Here is our valedictorian," said Mrs. Anderson, as Jonathan entered her physics classroom. The class erupted into applause. Jonathan was unaware of his surroundings. All except the new girl. There she sat, in the seat directly to his left. He noticed she kept looking at him with a look of familiarity. As if she had known him for a long time.

"So you're the Jonathan everyone keeps talking about. The smartest guy in the history of the school."

"I wouldn't say that," he said, blushing.

"Reagan," she said.

"Excuse me?"

"My name is Reagan."

"Nice to meet you."

"I'm your competition."

"That's good to know," Jonathan smirked.

"Mr. Bailey," said Mrs. Anderson. "Miss Peterson." The two students looked at each other with stiff smiles and quickly turned their attention to the front of the room. "You should focus on my teaching, and that goes double for you, Mr. Bailey," the teacher scolded them.

Overly embarrassed, Jonathan leaned forward on his desk. He was aware classmates were staring at him and he could feel his face turning red. He hid his face behind his backpack. Once Mrs. Anderson had her back to the class, Reagan slipped Jonathan a note. Realizing that the class had taken their attention off him, he could feel his face coming back to normal. He carefully unfolded the note but before he could read it, he was startled once again by the mysterious voice.

"We need to prepare you for the task at hand." The words seemed to come out of nowhere.

"I'm going crazy," Jonathan thought. "I'm a senior in high school, and I'm going absolutely, certifiably crazy."

Jonathan gave Mrs. Anderson an excuse, and got a pass to the bathroom. Locked inside a stall, he was in an absolute panic. "What do you want from me," he asked under his breath. "Why is this happening?" After what seemed an eternity, Jonathan exited the stall and began washing his face at the sink.

"Well, look at Mr. I have a fancy car," Michael said as he walked into the boy's room.

"Not now," Jonathan said, as he splashed water on his face. "Not now."

"You're not giving me lip, are you? Ferrari or not, I'll still kick your….."

"Is there a problem," interrupted a strange voice. Jonathan dried his face with a paper towel.

"No," Michael said. "We're doing just fine."

"No, sir," chided the strange voice.

"Yes, sir," Michael said. "I mean no, sir. No problem here, sir."

"Then get to class," said the man. Michael exited the bathroom as quickly as he had entered it. "Don't worry about him, Jonathan. I'll take care of him," the man told him.

"Do I know you?" Jonathan asked.

"Daniel Smith. I am a new substitute."

Jonathan hesitated, and then asked him, "How did you know my name?"

"Word travels fast," Mr. Smith said as he left the bathroom. "See you in class."

Jonathan stood looking in the mirror for a couple of minutes before heading back to class. As he entered the hallway, he stepped right into Krista's path.

"How is that for synchronicity?" Krista asked.

"Huh?" stuttered Jonathan.

"We were meant to run into each other," Krista said.

"And we almost did just that," he replied.

"Why aren't you in class?"

Jonathan answered, "Nature calls. Why were we supposed to run into each other?"

Both students were going to the science department.

"Movie night," Krista reminded him.

"Oh, yeah."

"Yes. You. Me. The movies."

"Tonight?"

"I'll be at your house at 7."

Jonathan walked along in awe, wondering if he was dreaming of if that conversation with Krista had really happened.

"You okay, Jonathan?" Mrs. Anderson asked, as he entered her classroom and took his seat. He nodded sheepishly and put his head down on his desk.

"Long time no see," Reagan said.

"Yes," he responded.

"You've missed most of class."

"My stomach. Must have been something I ate."

"What did you eat?"

"What's with all the questions?" Jonathan snapped.

"Just a concerned friend."

"Thanks."

"I wish you were feeling better," Reagan continued talking. "I was going to ask you to go to the football game with me tonight."

"Thanks, but I have something I have to do tonight," he answered.

"Maybe some other time."

After class as Jonathan was putting his books in his locker, someone grabbed him from behind. Without thinking, he grabbed both wrists and threw his opponent over his shoulder.

"What the Hell?" Charles said, surprised, having been caught off guard. He picked himself up off the floor and continued, "New car, new phone, and super human strength all in the same day?"

"Sorry about that," said his friend.

Chapter Three

Jonathan entered his last class of the day. Wouldn't you know…sitting right beside him: Reagan.

"Hello, stranger," she was the first to speak.

"Still here," Jonathan retorted.

"Good afternoon," Mr. Smith said. The substitute turned and wrote his name on the board.

"Good afternoon," the class said, in unison.

"Literature is about conversation." Mr. Smith began. "It's the reader having a conversation with the author. It's the material having a conversation with the reader. And it's the reader having a conversation with himself."

"Isn't he a substitute?" Reagan asked Jonathan, in a loud whisper.

"I think so."

"Don't tell me he's going to lecture us. Substitutes do not lecture. Don't they just give busy work?"

"I'm glad Reagan and Jonathan are already having a conversation. It seems rather thought provoking," Mr. Smith said.

"Sorry," the two teens replied in unison.

"No need to be sorry," said Mr. Smith. "This class is going to be a conversation. Since you seem quite comfortable with each other, you can pair up." As he paired up the other students, Reagan scooted her desk closer to Jonathan's.

"Let's have a conversation," Reagan began.

"Okay…."

"Favorite color?"

"I like them all."

"You sure you're not partial to black? As in a shiny new black Ferrari."

"Definitely one of my favorites."

"Favorite food?"

"Food in general."

"Ah, that's how it is. You're going to play hard to get. You're going to be Mr. Mysterious. Mr. Enigma. Mr. Sixty Four Dollar Question."

"I'm an open book," quipped Jonathan.

"How long have you been in Jacksonville?" Reagan continued.

"My whole life."

"Short and sweet."

"What?"

"Your answers. Short and sweet. Mr. Tough Nut to Crack."

"Ask me anything you want", Jonathan said.

"Tell me about your Mom."

"My Mom?"

"Anything I want, right?"

"She's great," he replied, thinking back on how strong she'd been since losing his father.

"What's great about her?"

"She's strong. She's tough. She's resilient."

"And your Dad?" Jonathan didn't speak. "You can learn a lot about someone by asking about their family.

"Continue." Reagan prodded.

"Next question."

"How about answering the Dad question first."

"What do you want to know?'

"What kind of man is he?"

"Enough about me," Jonathan said, cutting her off. Before Reagan could argue, the bell rang. "Saved by the bell." He gathered up his things.

"Nonsense," Reagan said, smiling. "We're just getting started.

Jonathan walked out of class and to his locker and Reagan followed.

"I'm being followed," he said.

"Yes," Reagan replied, "and I'm about to follow you to Burger House."

"Really…" he said somewhat sarcastically.

"Yes, we should go get a burger. I'm famished," she said, as if nobody else mattered.

Jonathan asked, "And I suppose we'll continue the conversation?"

"Exactly."

Jonathan opened his locker and started to put his books up when Krista snuck up behind him.

"You forget about tonight?" she asked, staring Reagan up and down.

"No," he replied, closing his locker.

"Good. I wouldn't want to have to come hunt you down."

"No need for that." He grinned.

"See you tonight then," Krista said as she turned and walked away.

"You're a busy man," Reagan said.

"That's what they say."

Burger House was crowded. It seemed like the whole town got hungry all at once. Jonathan arrived in the parking lot before Reagan. Before he got out of the car, his phone rang.

"Hello? Hey, Mom," he said.

"Where are you, Sweetheart?" Katherine asked.

"Waiting for a friend at Burger House. A new girl from school, and this place is packed," he told her. "Oh, and I have plans tonight, so you and Caroline can go to church without me."

"Okay, I have dinner ready," she said. "Was going to leave it in the oven for you.

Why don't you bring your friend here instead? I'd like to meet her."

"Okay, Mom. See you in a few minutes." When Reagan pulled in the parking lot Jonathan told her about the change in plans, and she followed him home. No sooner were they pulling in the driveway when Caroline came running out of the house. As she usually did, Caroline ran to her big brother and gave him a big hug. They both laughed as he grabbed her by the arms and began swinging her around in circles. Reagan retrieved her phone from her purse and started taking pictures of the two siblings. After playing with his sister for a few minutes, Jonathan introduced Caroline to Reagan. It was his turn to grab his phone and take pictures. He asked them to stand next to each other.

"You're cute," Reagan told Caroline. "Your brother has told me a lot about you."

"Did he tell you that he sleeps with a teddy bear?" Caroline asked. Reagan tried to hold her laughter in as she watched his face turn beet red. His precocious little sister began telling all sorts of interesting tidbits about Jonathan.

"That's enough," he told her, but he was laughing too.

Mrs. Bailey came outside and asked Jonathan,

"Aren't you going to introduce me to your new friend?"

"Yes, ma'am. This is Reagan Peterson."

"It's nice to meet you Mrs. Bailey," Reagan said. Caroline grabbed Reagan's hand and started pulling her into the house.

"Let's go play in my room," Caroline insisted. Katherine and Jonathan laughed as they watched the girls.

"Looks like you're not the only one with a new friend. Reagan seems like a nice young lady. Caroline really took to her. You should think about asking her out," his Mother suggested.

"I have a date with Krista tonight, Mom."

"Krista? The one I have heard about since you were kids? What are you two doing tonight?"

"Just going to a movie."

The kids washed their hands and the four of them sat down to dinner. Katherine and Caroline quickly ate and left to go to their church for a meeting. Reagan helped Jonathan clear off the table and the two of them sat on the front porch.

"I see you and my sister hit it off pretty well," Jonathan said.

"Yeah, she's really sweet," Reagan replied, smiling.

"She usually doesn't take to people that quickly." He didn't mind getting to know Reagan but he couldn't help but think about his date with Krista. He tried not to let it show and have a good time visiting with Reagan. He wanted to get to know her more.

"You've asked a lot of questions about me, Reagan, now tell me about you. How long have you lived in Jacksonville?"

"I just moved here. My Mother put me up for adoption when I was a baby. I live with a foster family." Jonathan could see the discomfort in her eyes.

"I'm sorry," he said.

"It's okay," Reagan replied. I try not to talk about it much. It's hard to move around to different families. I just try to take it one day at a time." Seeing Jonathan check his watch, she remembered he had plans. "I'd better be going. You have a date tonight and I have to be home soon. " He walked her to her car. "I hope we can do this again. Tell your Mom thanks for dinner."

"Sure," Jonathan smiled. As she opened the door, she turned around and looked Jonathan in the eyes. "You and Krista are going out tonight. Be careful. I don't know her at all, but I can feel that she is trouble." Before Jonathan could respond, she got in the car and he watched as she drove off. He stood there for a few minutes, with an uneasy feeling.

Chapter Four

Jonathan took a quick shower and dressed and putting his shoes on when the doorbell rang. "She's early," he thought to himself. He ran downstairs and opened the door. He couldn't believe it. There she was, the girl he had wanted to go out with for as long as he could remember.

"I know I'm early," Krista said. "I thought we could talk before going to the movie. You have a very nice house." She walked across the room and sat on the couch. Patting the seat beside her, she invited Jonathan to join her. He was nervous and was afraid that she would see that he was sweating. He slowly made his way to the couch, but as soon as he was within reach, Krista grabbed him, pulling him down beside her. She could tell his heart was racing. "What's the matter with you?" she asked him. "Calm down, I'm not going to hurt you." Trying to get him to relax, she looked around at the pictures on the walls. "Are those your mother and sister?" she asked.

Jonathan looked at the pictures and began to feel calmer. "Yes, that's them," he told her. I lost my father when I was young and they have been my whole world ever since. What about you and Michael?" he asked.

"Michael and I broke up back at the beginning of the summer." Krista slid closer to Jonathan. "All I see is him near you every time you make a move."

"Tell me, Krista, if you don't mind me asking. Why does someone like you decide to get together with someone like that?"

"We've been together for a long time. I guess he just grew on me. We decided after school let out that we'd stop seeing each other." Krista paused for a moment and continued, "Then last week he decided that we were serious again." Jonathan began to relax more as they talked. "Michael can be very physical when he gets upset. For one reason or another, he can't stand the sight of you." Making herself more comfortable, Krista turned towards Jonathan, putting her leg up on the couch. She could see he was more relaxed as she reached up and started running her fingers through his hair.

"Can I ask you another question?"

"Go ahead and ask," she answered. "What would you like to know?"

"Did you have anything to do with me getting attacked by Michael and his friends at the homecoming game last year?"

"I know your friend Charles has his own opinion about that, but let me explain.

No, I had nothing to do with that. Nothing at all. Michael did that all on his own. I remember that night really well, Jonathan. I saw it from a distance and tried to get closer to see what was going on. I saw you trying to run from them, but you were outnumbered. Then there was that loud lightning strike and everyone except you was lying on the ground. From where I was standing your eyes looked like they were golden, but that may have been because of the rain. Then Charles ran up behind you and shook you, and you came out of some kind of trance."

"I don't remember that night at all," said Jonathan, shaking his head. "Charles talks about it a lot but we never can figure it out."

Krista stood up and walked across the room to look at a picture on the wall.

"Who is the man in the black suit?" she asked. Jonathan walked over and stood next to her.

"That's my Uncle Philip. He works with the government and travels most of the time." Jonathan looked at his watch.

"We have plenty of time to make it to the theatre," Krista told him. Catching him off guard, she grabbed him in an embrace and began kissing him. Although Jonathan was shocked, he didn't pull away, instead kissing her back. He suddenly heard that voice again.

"No." he heard it intently. He pulled away from Krista.

"Not now!" he exclaimed. He repeated it a couple of times while pacing the floor. Krista was as shocked as he was.

"Are you okay or do you want to cancel our date?" she asked. She didn't know what to expect. Nobody had ever cancelled on her before.

"Certainly not," Jonathan yelled.

"Then why did you pull away from me?" she asked. She felt comfortable enough to slide closer to him, hoping to kiss him again. Jonathan responded to her touch and they leaned in towards each other. He wanted this as much as she did. He closed his eyes, but before he could feel her sweet lips against his, the voice said once again,

"No."

Jonathan pulled away again, but tried to play it off by suggesting they go ahead and go to the movie.

"Sure, we can go ahead and go if you want to," she told him. She was still a bit puzzled.

"I think it would be a good idea," he said smiling. He was still trying not to lose control. He didn't want to scare her away. However, he couldn't explain what was happening, because he didn't know himself. As he turned the lights off, Krista grabbed him again and tried to kiss him. This time he stopped her. "What's the matter with you?" he asked her. "This is not how I wanted our first date to be. I wanted us to talk like we were a few minutes ago and get to know each other better."

Krista was taken back by his reaction. "I can't believe this," she said. She had a stronger appreciation for Jonathan, as no other guy she dated ever respected her the way he did. As they walked to the car, he kept thinking about the voice and where it was coming from. He was pretty sure it all had something to do with the man in the vision he had early that morning. He opened the car door for Krista and asked her,

"What made you ask me out? Ever since we were kids you've never paid any attention to me, almost as if I didn't exist."

"I don't know why, Jonathan. Michael had a lot to do with that and I'm very sorry. He will always be a demanding person, but I'm done with him."

"Does Michael know where you are tonight?" asked Jonathan.

"I'm not sure, and anyways, I couldn't care less if he does. Let's not talk about him anymore, okay? This is our first date so let's just enjoy ourselves at the movie."

"That's a great idea", Jonathan said. "I'm tired of talking about him too." They both let out a sigh of relief.

Chapter Five

Krista led the way out of the theatre. She offered him her hand as she asked,

"That was a great movie, wasn't it?" He took her hand and they entwined fingers. On the way to the car, she spoke again. "I have a fun idea if you have time. There's a palm reader not too far from here. Let's go."

"Do you really think that's a good idea?" he said with obvious trepidation. He had a bad feeling about this.

"It's a great idea. Come on. You'll see how much fun it'll be. Wouldn't you like to hear about your future?" His bad feeling grew deeper, but he would do just about anything to make his date with Krista last longer. Jonathan took his phone out of his pocket and called home. His mom and sister weren't home yet, so he left a message. As they got in the car, he couldn't make the bad feelings go away. She continued, "We are going to have a good time at her house. Her name is Anita

McKnight and she's very good." Paying more attention to his gut feeling than to what she was saying, he interrupted her.

"Where does this woman live?" he questioned.

"She has a place way out in the country," Krista answered. "Do you know where Lakeview is, out past the cemetery?"

"I've heard of it, but never been out that far."

"Well, relax and live a little," she said. She reached up and rubbed the back of his neck. "Don't be afraid." Although his skin tingled at the feel of her hand on his neck, he still could not shake the uneasy feeling. "Jonathan, how long have you liked me?" she asked.

"For as long as I can remember, Krista," he began. "Since we were little kids back in grade school. I've always liked you, but when we started the 9th grade, you changed. Michael came along and you started treating me different. Suddenly it was as if I no longer existed." His voice started to get louder. "Explain it to me," he demanded.

"What happened? We were friends all the way up to the 8th grade. Was it because Michael was a freshman varsity star? These past few years you have turned me down, time and time again. Now look at us. Suddenly we're at the movies. Want to explain that to me, because I'm confused," he exclaimed. They sat for a couple of minutes in silence. Finally, Krista found the courage to speak.

"Jonathan, I told you I was sorry. Do you think I don't know what a big mistake I made? I remember how sweet you were to me, ever since we met. All the poetry books you've given me, and all the songs you wrote."

"Then what was it?" he asked impatiently. "I liked you a lot, thought about you all the time. You were it for me. But my heart suffered. I even went against my best friend. Charles always told me that you were a fraud."

"I'm sorry, Jonathan, what can I do to make this hurt go away?" she asked. "We are together now and the only thing we can do is start over. If you can give me another chance. Remember when we used to throw rocks at cars as they drove by?"

"Yeah, I remember," he answered, almost in a whisper.

"Give me a chance to show myself worthy and we can have all that back."

Krista turned the car into the psychic's driveway. Jonathan slowly got out of the car. The sick feeling just would not go away. He wasn't sure what he imagined, yet seemed surprised that the house looked normal from the outside. They went through the gate and walked across the yard and up to the front door.

"Trust me," Krista urged him. "Let's go in and you'll see that everything will be okay." Jonathan was still reluctant, but she had already rung the bell, so he figured there was no backing out. Krista whispered in his ear as the door opened, "Just relax, okay?"

Jonathan found himself face to face with Miss Anita McKnight. Krista was the first to speak. "Hey Anita, how are you tonight?" she asked.

After sizing up the two teenagers, she replied.

"I'm doing fine. Why didn't you call before coming over here?"

"I'm sorry about that, but I have a friend who wants to have his palm read. You can also tell him his future. And, by the way, skepticism is his middle name." Jonathan finally found his voice, and clearing his throat said,

"Hello, my name is Jonathan and I am a friend of Krista's."

"So, you don't believe in this type of thing?" Anita asked, still looking him over, trying to size him up.

"I'm not saying that I don't. But my family raised me different and I've never had this done before," he replied. "I'm guessing it won't hurt anything to give it a try."

"Krista, you stay in here and Jonathan you come with me," she said, leading him towards the back of the house.

"This is a nice house, Miss McKnight. I sort of pictured it to be an old, dark, scary house," he admitted.

"No, that's just the way you see them in movies," she said as she opened a door and motioned for him to go in. "Did you think I'd be an old decrepit woman wearing black flowing clothes?"

"Yes, ma'am, you could say that," he said.

"You're a well-mannered young man. I like that. I don't get that very often around here."

"Yes, ma'am, that's how I was raised. My mother wouldn't have it any other way. Miss McKnight, you look very young. How old are you?" he asked her.

"That's a good question, Son." The psychic smiled. "But I won't answer it." She pointed to a chair, and he sat down while she took a seat across the table from him.

"Please try to calm down and relax. First, I'll read your palm, and then I'll tell you your future. Let me see your hand."

He wasn't quite sure what to think as he nervously stretched his arm across the table and she began studying his palm. Just as Jonathan saw a look in her eyes that he had never seen before, the table started shaking and the mirrors hanging on the walls all shattered. The look in her eyes grew more intense as she looked up and stared at Jonathan. "I want you to listen to me very carefully. What I am about to tell you is very important," she said. "You have an ancient power within you that's been lying dormant. It's as if you are two different people. This power is well over ten thousand years old." Trembling, Jonathan stood up and tried to run out of the room. Anita grabbed him by the arm.

"What do you mean "ancient power?" he asked the psychic.

"You must listen to me! Your family is in grave danger. They are being attacked at this very moment. You must hurry home, their lives depend on it!" With those words, she pushed him towards the door.

"Krista, let's go. NOW!" he yelled as he ran for the front door. She followed him out into the yard. "Give me your keys, I'll drive."

"Jonathan, take my keys and go. Don't worry about me. Just go if you have to."

"That's ridiculous, Krista! Why would I take your car and leave you here? Come on, let's go!"

They got in the car, and he sped out of there. With emergency flashers on and blowing the horn as he flew through intersections, he didn't care if any cop saw him. He was not stopping until he got home. He took his cell phone out of his pocket and repeatedly tried to call his house. Nobody ever answered. Krista tried to talk to him.

"What's the matter, Jonathan?" she asked. "What did she say that made you so upset? Where are we going?" Jonathan kept driving like there was no tomorrow. Krista stared at him, and wondered if he even knew she was in the car with him. When they got to his house, he didn't take time to pull in the driveway.

He stopped the car in front of the house and as he got out and ran towards the house, he yelled back at Krista.

"Go home!" he yelled. "Go home!"

Jonathan ran into the house screaming. "Mom! Caroline! Where are you? Hello?" He started up the stairs taking them two at a time, when halfway up he stopped as he noticed a wallet on one of the steps. He stuck it in his pocket and ran upstairs, still screaming. As he got to the top of the stairs, he heard what sounded like a man in a lot of pain. He ran into his mother's bedroom to find both her and Caroline lying on the floor. He checked their pulses, but there was none to be found. Jonathan was crying, tears pouring down his face. Knowing there was no hope, he screamed as loud as he could, "Somebody help me!" He had forgotten about the man he had heard until he heard him try to speak. He looked across the room to find a man lying in a pool of blood with a gunshot wound in his side. The man could hardly breathe, but managed to tell Jonathan that his family had been poisoned with strychnine. Jonathan went over and tried to shake the man. "What happened here? I want to know who did this," Jonathan demanded.

Between labored breaths, the man tried to warn him.

"There's a bomb hooked to your gas line. You need to get out of here. There's not much time before it explodes!" Those were the man's last words. Jonathan sat back and stared at his mother and sister for a few seconds then ran bawling downstairs. Not knowing what he expected to find or what he planned to do, he ran to the basement. The bomb was right there in plain sight, but the timer only had 5 seconds remaining. Jonathan knew this was it; he could not make it out. He felt someone grab him, and saw a bright light as he blacked out from the force of the explosion.

Chapter Six

A man stood over Jonathan as he lay passed out on a cot. "We have a lot of work to do, Maximus, before we can go attack Dmitri," the man said. Maximus was a cheetah from the future. He was here in this time to prepare Jonathan for the task he was needed to do. Maximus was chief of all the animals in the future. "When Jonathan wakes up we'll take him through everything that has happened and why."

Jonathan woke to find himself in a strange room. Somewhere he had never been before. He tried to sit up but the pain was too intense and he lay back down. He let his eyes focus a few minutes before looking around the room, trying to figure out where he was and what was happening. He recognized the man in the room with him.

"Hey, you're that substitute teacher from school," he exclaimed. "What happened and where am I?"

"First of all, Jonathan," Daniel Smith started to explain. "I want to say how sorry I am about your family." Jonathan suddenly remembered the events from earlier. He dropped his head and his eyes became moist. "Secondly," Daniel continued, "You're going to have to listen very carefully to what I'm about to tell you. I know you have been through a lot tonight, but you need to put your feelings aside. The world is depending on you." Jonathan stared at him, confused. "Son, we have a lot to go over and not much time in which to do it. This won't make sense to you right now, but your body has two inhabitants. You and Dexter."

"Who is Dexter and what on earth are you talking about?" Jonathan demanded to know. His head was already spinning from the pain and hearing this unbelievable story was almost too much.

Daniel went on to explain, "Dexter is the first born son of the great wizard Darius. Darius is the keeper of the golden dragon, which is known as the Dragon of Supremacy. His brother, Dmitri is the keeper of the black dragon, known as the Dragon of Treachery. We believe Dmitri is responsible for what happened to your family. According to the scrolls, their father vanished and was never heard from again. Dmitri is a greedy man and wants nothing more than to also master the golden dragon. Because of the impurity of his heart, he could not even touch the golden box. Dmitri acted fast in blowing up your house. It doesn't make sense. We're trying to investigate and figure out what he's doing and why. He must have known that Dexter is using your body, and came here and found a body of his own to occupy. Dmitri is alive and active while unfortunately for you, Dexter is still dormant. There is a necklace I will give you later. When Dexter comes alive the necklace will shatter and the golden dragon will be unleashed." Daniel was talking so fast that Jonathan's head was spinning as he tried hard to take it all in.

"Could this really be happening," he thought to himself. Aloud he asked, "So, are you the one I saw this morning and kept hearing all day today?"

"Yes, son. That was me," he answered. "We have a lot to do to prepare you and we're running short on time. Your times here are different."

"Different?" Jonathan asked, confused. "What do you mean different?" Daniel turned to face him.

"One month as you know it is really only about a day long to us," he said. "I know it's hard to understand, but we really don't have a lot of time." Jonathan, feeling dumbfounded, sat in silence. His thoughts were so intermingled that it felt like they were beating against the sides of his head. All that had happened today and there was more? This was all so overwhelming. And what exactly was it they were expecting from him? These were just a few of the thoughts racing through his mind, repeatedly. He almost felt like he would pass out again. He suddenly realized Daniel was still talking to him.

"You have some pretty intense training to get through. There is speed, combat and vehicle training. Not to mention some classroom time. Come. Let's take a walk, and I'll show you around the mansion." His legs still a bit shaky, Jonathan stood up slowly and tried to keep up with Daniel. As they walked through a doorway, Jonathan heard a familiar voice.

"Daniel, what do you want me to do next?" asked the voice. Jonathan turned around and found himself staring into the face of Reagan.

"Reagan?" he exclaimed, surprised. "What are you doing here? What do you have to do with all of this?"

"We don't have time for a lot of chit chat, we have work to do. Reagan, you're welcome to join us as I show Jonathan around," Daniel said. She quickly followed behind them. Daniel led them to a door that went outside. He opened it, but made sure Jonathan didn't go out. "Let me explain," he began. "Our gravity is twice what you're used to. And you will have to run out there. So stay inside until we know you can handle it." Jonathan nodded and looked out the open door. Off in the distance he could see a mountain. He could tell there was a big entryway on the side of the mountain. Noticing what he was seeing, Daniel told him about the mountain.

"That is Aqueous Cave and we will go there as soon as you are ready. You, and you alone, will go to the center of it. Follow me and I will show you the combat chamber where you will train." As they walked, Jonathan could feel Reagan's stare. Feeling uncomfortable, realizing he did not really know her at all, he angrily told her to stop.

"Where did you go that night, Jonathan… that kept you from being at home with your family?" Daniel asked.

"I went to a movie with a friend and then she took me to a psychic's house," Jonathan answered. He went on to say, "She told me the same thing you did, about there being some power or something living inside of me. This Dexter, how powerful is he? Moreover, why me? And what is the big deal about waking him up at this very moment in time? And do you have any idea who this bad guy is living in?"

"We have a lot to explain to you, Jonathan. Dexter has been inside you since you were born. He is very wise and powerful, and the reason you are so intelligent. When I said earlier that our world was depending on you, truthfully, the fate of the world is in yours and Dexter's hands alone. The things you are about to learn can only be learned by you. Nobody else can learn them. Since Dexter is inside you, that will give you special abilities too," Daniel told him. They arrived at the combat chamber. Daniel continued to explain. Jonathan wondered how he would remember all of this, let alone fulfill all the tasks that they expected of him. "This is a very unique combat training course. You will be at the maximum level which is twenty-twenty."

"Okay," Jonathan said, hesitantly. "What exactly is twenty-twenty?"

"As I said, it's the maximum level. You will be trained by holograms and they will be traveling at the speed of light," said Daniel.

"There's no way I can do that," Jonathan argued.

"Yes you can! And you will," Daniel assured him. "I know this is too much to grasp all at once, but you're going to have to trust yourself. Remember what I said. Dexter is inside you, and because of his power your body will be able to withstand this kind of pressure. You'll see."

"Tell me more about these holograms you mentioned," Jonathan said.

"They are very fast. Like I said, they move at the speed of light. You will have to focus. Don't worry; they will be in the form of men, so you will recognize their shape. You will learn to channel all your thoughts and energy into what you are doing if you ever expect to hit them. Jonathan, when you are able to do this, along with the added strength you get from Dexter, no one will be able to stand against you. Not even Dmitri. There are also weapons you will have to learn. Some are similar to weapons that you know, so you will recognize their looks. Others will be new to you. Come; let's go to the vehicle room. Reagan, it's almost time for lunch. You'll take care of that for us, won't you?" Reagan nodded, and walked away. Jonathan watched her walk off and then turned to Daniel, "You never answered my question about the brother. Who's body do you think Dmitri is using here?" Jonathan stopped, which made Daniel do the same and face Jonathan.

"We don't know yet. We've been too busy tracking you." Daniel admitted.

"Whoever it is, that person is also powerful. The thing is, the brothers are different. Dexter is in you, but did not take control of you. You two are still separate beings. Whoever Dmitri is occupying, we're sure he has taken total control of that person." I will explain more when we get to the classroom. And eventually everything will be explained to you." As they approached another door, Daniel stopped. "This is it," he nodded to Jonathan. "I'm sure you'll like what you see in here. But first, there is more I need to explain to you. You and Reagan are the only two people who can access this room. Not even I can, as I choose to keep it that way."

"Why just us?" Jonathan asked. He was confused, but at the same time found all of this to be interesting. He tried to stay down to earth by reminding himself that there was a task he had to perform and he wasn't too sure what to make of all this yet. Many of Daniel's warnings kept repeating themselves in his mind.

"The only way to open this door is through that panel you see there on the wall," Daniel pointed to a control panel on the wall. "It's a scanner and it uses retinal recognition. Reagan designed it and the only ones that really need access to this room are you and Dexter. When you look into the scanner it will scan both yours and Dexter's retinas."

"Really?" Jonathan grinned.

"Go ahead. Look into the scanner," urged Daniel. Jonathan leaned in and put his face as close to the scanner as he could get. He jumped slightly as the laser came across his line of vision. The door opened and seeing the inside made Jonathan's eyes light up like a Christmas tree. He suddenly forgot all this talk about good and evil, tasks and lessons. He felt almost like a kid at Christmas. Daniel paid attention to which vehicle Jonathan was looking at the most. "What you see is the golden lion. At the push of a button, it becomes the golden eagle or golden badger. The motorcycle beside it is the golden leopard and at the push of a button, it becomes the golden manta ray. These vehicles are very fast and cannot be detected on any radar."

"That's amazing! Incredible!" Jonathan exclaimed. He circled both vehicles many times trying to take in every detail. He was anxious to drive them both, but did not dare say so aloud. He knew there were more important things that needed to be done. He knew the time would come.

Jonathan noticed Daniel heading towards another door on the other side of the room. He quickly followed. "Where does this door lead?" he asked.

"The classroom is in here," Daniel replied. "But that isn't where we're headed just yet. Follow me to the second door and you'll have to have your eyes scanned again." Jonathan felt a bit important, as he was the only one who could open the door. Walking into the hall, he saw that it was filled with all sorts of weapons: guns, knives, weapons he had no idea what they were. They were hanging on the walls and in glass cases. He had never seen so many weapons at one time.

"Wow," said Jonathan. "All these are at my disposal?"

"Yes, they are," Daniel answered. "And when your training is complete, you will know how to use each and every one of them. Jonathan, your natural abilities will benefit you greatly, but with Dexter you have supernatural abilities which will help you to handle these weapons and vehicles." As they got to the end of the hall there was a doorway leading to a room with tables and chairs. "Let's have a seat and talk," said Daniel. Jonathan sat down and watched as Daniel picked up a gold box from a desk and came and sat down across the table from him. He showed the box to Jonathan. It had a golden shine that was almost blinding. Daniel placed it on the table and opened it. "This box is very similar to the one that holds the spirit of the Supremacy Dragon," Daniel said, pulling a necklace out of the box. "This necklace is for you to wear. When Dexter awakens, the necklace will shatter and the box with the dragon will open. At that time, the dragon's spirit will enter into you and will give you unimaginable power. Jonathan gazed at the necklace. It had a golden half-moon, and looked very familiar to him. They were interrupted as Reagan entered the room and announced that lunch was ready.

"We'll be there in a minute," Daniel told her. Reagan nodded and walked out of the room, leaving the two men to finish talking. Daniel looked at Jonathan. "I know a lot of this sounds odd to you and may be hard to believe. These things don't just happen to be here. You are a very wealthy young man, Jonathan. Every time any money is dropped anywhere in the world, it disappears there and appears in your bank account here in the mansion." Jonathan looked perplexed.

"What exactly does that mean for me?" he asked.

"Actually, it means that you are a billionaire," Daniel replied. Reagan and I handle the finances concerning the mansion, but it's mostly taken care of by her. There is an ATM here that will be available to you. It uses the same retina scanner that you have used to open doors. C'mon. Let's go get something to eat." Jonathan followed Daniel to the kitchen. Reagan was still preparing the table. She and Jonathan locked eyes until he crossed the table and sat down.

"Everything looks nice and the food smells great. Nice job, Reagan," said Jonathan, realizing how hungry he was.

"Thank you," was all she said, and they all began to eat.

"So tell me, how long was I being watched?" Jonathan asked.

"Ever since you were little, probably about 7 or 8 years old. We watched your activities mainly to see if Dexter would wake up while you were still too young to understand all of this. No matter the connection between the two of you, there is no way you could have understood his power or been capable of handling it. By the way, when Dexter does wake up you two will be able to communicate with each other. Every night the necklace lights up. That's an indication that it is time to begin your training."

"I thought you said Dmitri was already awake and active," Jonathan questioned. Daniel continued to explain.

"Dmitri is awake. We are sure of that because of the necklaces. Your necklace doubles in brightness whenever it's near the black one. Each time your necklace shatters, it fixes itself once the dragons come out of their boxes. Both dragons return to their respective boxes once they are finished. From then on, you and Dexter will control when he needs to emerge."

"So this necklace can tell whenever Dexter is active?" Jonathan asked.

"Yes," Daniel answered. "It's indicating that the time is drawing near. That is why we have to hurry up and prepare you. We are afraid that pretty soon Dmitri's host body will do something to reveal himself. When that happens you have to be ready to move, whether or not Dexter is awake. I hope that he will awaken while you are in battle, if not before then. We are hoping it's before then. Regardless of how soon all this takes place, you have exactly a month to prepare to enter the Aqueous Cave to retrieve the fiery swords and the mystic medallion." Jonathan had so many questions, but did not want to interrupt. Daniel would answer them all in time. "I know you're curious about the medallion and swords; let me explain. The swords are fire swords. They burn with extreme temperatures that only Dexter's power can withstand. The medallion is pure diamond and will enable you to speak to individuals from another realm. Namely, you from the future, a thousand years from now, to be exact. When you die your spirit will find another host body."

"This is all way too much for me to handle," Jonathan said, feeling somewhat uneasy.

"I know," Daniel nodded. "But there's a lot you have to know about yourself in addition to all you have to learn in order to complete your task. You cannot just learn how to do battle. You must understand what is happening and how all this came to be and how it got to this point. We do not have much time, but I will try to take it one step at a time. I know how overwhelming all of this is for you."

Jonathan got up from the table and walked out onto the patio. Daniel watched him and when he was sure the young man was out of ear shot, he turned to Reagan.

"Don't let your personal feelings get in the way, Reagan. You cannot become involved with him. Not now. His mind must stay clear of all distractions. He is going to really need to focus. Denying what I am saying would be lying."

"I know, and I will not deny it," Reagan said. "But Jonathan has been a part of my life for a long time, even if he doesn't know it. Remember, Daniel, we've been tracking him since he was a young boy."

Daniel quickly replied. "Consider your age, Reagan. You are thirty eight and he is only eighteen. Listen to me. All I'm saying is if you are interested in him, wait until this is over before you try to pursue him." They became quiet as Jonathan came back in and sat back down at the table. Daniel and Reagan both knew what was on his mind and waited for him to tell them. However, he never did. He hurriedly finished his dinner and excused himself from the table saying,

"Good night. I will see you in the morning. Would one of you please show me where my room is?" Before Daniel could respond, Reagan jumped up.

"I'll show you, Jonathan. Follow me." As they left the room, Daniel shook his head, figuring Reagan had not heard a word of what he had just told her. "Are you okay?" Reagan asked Jonathan as they were going up the stairs.

"Yes; I'm just shocked, amazed and tired." When they reached the top of the stairs, they both stopped and looked at each other. Jonathan started to cry. "You know, Reagan, my family really liked you." She grabbed him and gave him a big hug. She kept her hands on his waist.

"When Caroline dragged me upstairs to her room, she told me that she'd always wanted a big sister. Jonathan, I want you to know how tremendously that touched me."

"Thank you for being here for me now," he said, looking into her eyes.

"I'll be here for you throughout your training. It won't be easy, but I know you'll do just fine," she reassured him.

"I hope so," he replied. "I've got to do this for my family. They didn't deserve to be murdered." They let go of each other and headed down the hall. She led him to his room and Jonathan went in without saying another word. Reagan wanted desperately to follow him, to comfort him. But remembering what Daniel had said, she stopped herself. Jonathan closed the door, sat on the bed, and cried. After a few minutes, he dried his eyes and lay down. His mind filled with wonderful memories of his family, many of them of good times with his dad. His eyes started to tear up again. He made a silent plea to Dexter.

"If you can help me, please, I'm begging you to please help me get revenge.

Caroline was so young and they were good people. They did not deserve this. Please if you wake up within me, I want revenge!" That was his last thought before drifting off to sleep.

Chapter Seven

Reagan and Daniel sat at the table and discussed the situation concerning Jonathan. Reagan was the first to speak.

"Do you think Jonathan will be able to handle all of this that's ahead of him?" she asked.

"We'll just have to wait and see," Daniel replied. He looked off in the distance.

"He will need stamina and durability, but Dexter can only give him those things if he's awake. I am more worried about the task awaiting him in the Aqueous Cave than the training. The power that Dexter possesses is more than Jonathan can imagine. Greater than his brother's. But Jonathan will have to be sharp and willing to be put in tough positions or things won't go well." The worry in his brow showed more prominently as he spoke. "Whoever did this to his family must have some knowledge of who Jonathan is. We just don't understand why they didn't go directly after Jonathan. Going after his family just does not make sense. They posed no threat of danger to anyone."

"It all seems odd to me," Reagan said, shaking her head. "Killing his family and blowing up the house. Why blow up the house? Were they trying to get rid of any evidence? And what about Jonathan, did they know he would come home in time to see it all happen and not be able to do anything?"

"That's a good question, Reagan," Daniel said. "I guess we'll find that out as time goes by. You may need to see what you can find out on the street where the house was. It was at night, but there was a lot of activity so maybe someone saw or heard something. I don't like it, but we may have to discuss this with Jonathan."

"I know," said Reagan, nodding her head. "But he's been through so much tonight." Daniel noticed in the tone of her voice that she was depressed, and was faced once again with her feelings for Jonathan. He thought before he spoke, choosing his words carefully.

"Remember what we talked about, Reagan, and don't lose your focus. I know you two will be around each other a lot, you will become his adviser and accountant and help him in battle. But Jonathan lost his family and needs to mourn and heal."

"I know," she agreed. "Spending that little bit of time around his family, I saw so much love between them. He loved them dearly, and adored his sister.

"You need to put your feelings aside, and realize that's what's going to drive him to seek revenge. Make no mistake, Reagan, we are racing against time to prepare him. We only have 3 days. According to the scrolls, once the keeper has obtained Dexter's host, the conflict must happen after the 3rd sunset."

"Do the scrolls say anything about who will be the victor?" Reagan asked.

"No, they don't," he answered. "That part of the scrolls was lost somewhere in time. We have to prepare Jonathan the best we can. This battle will take place whether or not Dexter awakens. With Dmitri having the power of the Black Dragon of Treachery, he and his host will be invisible to Jonathan unless Dexter is there to help him. The battle will not last long if that's the case, and Jonathan will lose. I cannot stress enough that the fate of our world lies in Dexter's hands. The only reason Dmitri did not take over the world then was that he was forced into a cocoon state for three thousand years.

He had killed his father and drowned Dexter."

"Wait a minute," Reagan interrupted. "I thought if a wizard killed another wizard they couldn't be revived."

"That's only true with magic," Daniel explained to her. "He killed their father with magic, but drowned Dexter. Their spirits then travel around in search of the perfect host body. They must see something in that person that is in direct likeness of themselves."

"So that's why Dexter chose Jonathan?" Reagan asked.

"We believe that since he was a wizard of humility, that must be what he saw in Jonathan. They are so similar in that respect, which would explain the magnitude of Dexter's powers. It would also explain why Dmitri would be so determined to get rid of Jonathan before Dexter awakens. I still don't understand the reason for blowing up the house. He could not have known that Jonathan would return home at that very moment to find his family dead. If he hadn't come home then, he may never have known what happened to them. Reagan, I need you to always expect the unexpected. To be so close to Jonathan, he will have to trust you completely. For all we know, one of his friends could be behind all of this."

"Can you tell me what exactly is going to happen when Dexter awakens and summons the Golden Dragon of Supremacy?" Reagan was curious to know.

"That has never happened before, so there's no way to know exactly," Daniel responded. "But rest assured, when this does take place, the universe will know. I'm going to bed. I

suggest you do the same. We have a busy schedule tomorrow."
He scooted his chair back, stood up and left the room. Reagan
remained at the table for a while, alone with her thoughts.
Unable to sort out everything in her mind that they had talked
about, she gave up and headed upstairs to her room. She
hesitated as she passed Jonathan's door. Figuring he was
already asleep, she was surprised to hear noise coming from
inside. Wondering what she was hearing, she put her ear up to
the door, convincing herself that it was just concern for him.
She reminded herself that Daniel was right when he said they
all needed to focus on the next 3 days. Realizing that what she
was hearing was Jonathan murmuring and that it was getting
louder, Reagan slowly opened the door. She found him in the
middle of a nightmare. Just as she entered the room, Jonathan
shouted out.

"Mom, Caroline! I'm on my way. Hold on!" Reagan
quietly inched her way to the foot of his bed, not wanting to
wake him up. Suddenly Jonathan rose up and she saw that he
was drenched in sweat. She saw a shine in the darkness as she
realized there was light pulsating from his eyes. They were
golden, as if there were fire in them. As quickly as she noticed
it, his eyes returned to normal and Jonathan woke up. Seeing
her standing at the foot of his bed startled him and he asked her,
"What are you doing in here?"

"I'm sorry, Jonathan. I didn't mean to frighten you," she started. I heard you talking in your sleep, and I was worried about you. I just meant to check on you without waking you if I could. I'm sorry." With those words, Reagan headed for the door.

"No, wait. Please don't go," Jonathan cried out. As she stopped and turned around, he continued. "Please sit down and let's talk. I really don't want to be alone right now." The two of them sat on the bed and Jonathan began to cry. "It's just not fair!

My family did not deserve this. Whatever all of this is about, they did not know anything and could have been left alone! Whoever did this didn't care about them at all, but I did! They were my family. I swear I'll get revenge if I ever find out who did this." Jonathan leaned over and put his head on Reagan's shoulder and she, in turn, put her arm around him, and slowly began running her fingers through his hair.

"Jonathan, if you can trust me to help you, I will do anything I can. I will be with you through all of this. I know you're hurting and I know it's not fair to tell you not to be angry, but we need to remain focused on what we all have to do. I am not trying to dismiss what you're feeling, I really do understand, but your anger could have an effect on when Dexter wakes up. I know you haven't known me for very long, but I know you. I have watched you since you were a young kid and you mean something to me. Tell me, how long have you felt like you were different? I remember that growing up you sometimes had feelings of inadequacy." Jonathan thought about her question before he answered.

"There were many times I felt different because I would get great bursts of energy that seemed to come out of nowhere. Sometimes when I would get angry things would happen. I cannot explain them but they were phenomenal. I blacked out a lot, I guess because of Dexter's power." They both got quiet for a few minutes when Jonathan finally broke the silence. "If you don't mind me asking, Reagan, how old are you?" Knowing how strong her feelings were for him, Reagan hesitated.

"I'm thirty eight years old," she finally answered. Jonathan acted as if he was in shock and rolled off the bed, ending up sitting on the floor.

"You're thirty eight years old?" he gasped. "You don't look any older than I am, maybe even younger. That's amazing how you sat in class and made yourself look so young." Blushing from the compliments, Reagan joined him on the floor and jumped on top of him, pushing him back so he was lying on the floor. Looking down at him with her hair in his face and laughing, she asked.

"Is that a problem for you, my being older?" Jonathan quit laughing as he moved the hair from her face, searching for her eyes.

"No that's not a problem," he replied. Reagan scooted back enabling her to pull him up to a sitting position and they sat face to face, gazing into each other's eyes. After a few seconds, she pulled Jonathan to her and their lips met. Getting lost in the moment, Reagan suddenly realized he was getting too deep into the moment. She pulled away. Reagan stood up first and at the same time they both said, "I'm sorry."

"We have to put any feelings we have aside and focus on the mission. Remember, you have a planet to save," she told Jonathan. "We wouldn't want to do anything that might jeopardize the situation." Not really hearing a word she said, Jonathan reached for her hand and spoke.

"This would be my first time," he said, sounding a bit anxious.

"Really?" Reagan truly was surprised. "I guess I figured you and what's her name had been together. The one you went to the movie with that night." She gave him a look of disappointment and turned away.

"You mean Krista?" Jonathan asked. "You must not have watched me too closely or you'd have known she's always been with Michael. We've only kissed and that was that same day at my house." This conversation brought back to mind the chaos of that evening. He hung his head and sighed. Sorrow quickly turning to anger, he clenched his fists and said, "We will get to the bottom of this, whatever this is. I need to know who did this to my family and why. I need to know! Reagan, I promise you I will give this mission my all! Hopefully the three of us will be able to wake Dexter, release this Golden Dragon and defeat Dmitri." Reagan nodded and stood up.

"It's time we were both getting to bed," she said. "We have a big day tomorrow and you especially need to get your rest."

"You're right," he replied. "I do need to get some sleep so my first day won't be my worst day." Reagan left his room and Jonathan lay down with his head resting on his hands for a few minutes before turning off the light.

Chapter Eight

When Jonathan woke up the next morning Reagan was standing at the foot of his bed holding clothes for him to wear.

"Good morning," she said. "Were you able to sleep after I left you last night?"

Jonathan got out of bed and stood there stretching.

"Good morning," he said. "Yeah, I guess I finally got some sleep last night. You did help me to relax a bit." Reagan tried to hide the smile on her face behind the clothes. Reaching out to take the clothes, Jonathan asked, "Are those for me? Good grief! These are heavy! How much do they weigh?" It was a rhetorical question, not one he really expected an answer to, so he was surprised when she responded.

"They are about twenty five pounds," Reagan said. "They are necessary for your training, and will benefit you greatly."

"Twenty five pounds?" Jonathan exclaimed. "How is it that you're not straining carrying them?"

"Don't think that just because I'm a woman that I'm weak. Remember what happened to you last night?" She walked behind him and gave him a friendly shove with her shoulder. Grinning at him, she added, "Don't you ever forget it." With that being said, she walked out of the room.

Before Jonathan was completely dressed, Daniel entered his room.

"Doesn't anyone knock around here?" Jonathan asked. Daniel nodded.

"Remember that this is a very important day, Jonathan. It may not come easy to you right away, but just do your best. No doubt today will be your hardest but we have to work fast." Daniel led him out the door and they headed down the hall.

"Remember, we have three weeks to prepare before you have to enter the Aqueous Cave."

At the bottom of the stairs, Reagan met them and handed Jonathan 2 slices of wheat bread. Bewildered, he looked first at the bread, then at Reagan, then Daniel.

"This is all I get for breakfast?" he queried. Reagan answered.

"You will find this bread is not like what you are used to. It has all the vitamins and minerals you get in a normal human breakfast. Sorry we are rushing you. We've already eaten." Jonathan grabbed the bread and began eating as he followed the others down the hall, struggling in the strange clothes. They walked to the patio and Daniel stopped.

"This will be your conditioning," he said. He motioned for Jonathan to step on out. Upon reaching the patio, the young man fell to the ground hard. It was a struggle to get back to his feet but he managed it. He felt stiff, but in these heavy clothes he could barely stand, let alone stretch.

"This is how I'm supposed to train?" Jonathan asked.

"Most certainly," Daniel replied, looking serious. "You'll do just fine. Remember, just do your best and keep trying. Pointing to a trail, he continued, "Just try to run a mile."

"That's crazy," Reagan interjected. "Daniel, do you realize he weighs about two hundred and fifty pounds, at least?"

"Yes, Reagan, I realize that," he answered. "We knew this wasn't going to be a cake walk. This is his first day, but I do not need to remind you that what time we have to prepare him is precious. He is already standing and that's because of Dexter."

"As far as his power goes, I think we may be overlooking something," Reagan remarked. Daniel nodded and looked at Jonathan.

"Go ahead and try to run," he told him. Jonathan struggled once again but he managed a labored run.

"He's slow, but at least he's moving," said Reagan.

"Just watch, he'll speed up," Daniel responded. As Jonathan slowly became accustomed to the weight of the clothes, he could tell he was moving faster. That served as motivation, until he realized the bushes along the trail were moving. Assuming he was alone on the trail, it startled him and he stopped. As he watched the bushes, he found himself more curious than anything. He was startled once again when a small cheetah came out of the bushes and ran right in Jonathan's direction. It was harder to start running from a dead stop, but he couldn't just stand there, so he started running. Fear welled up inside him, as he knew he couldn't outrun a cheetah, even without all the added weight he was carrying. He was exhausted, but elated to see the cheetah run past him and out of sight. He stopped in his tracks, and as the adrenaline slowed down, his legs felt like jelly and his arms seemed to be melting from fatigue. Waiting for his legs to rest, he looked around and at his surroundings. The mansion was only about a quarter of a mile away, but seemed unreachable. He noticed the cheetah standing on the patio with Daniel and Reagan. His mind suddenly went back to the night before when he found his family and he remembered how helpless he felt. Looking again at the patio, knowing that was his immediate goal, he shouted out.

"I won't give up!" With those words came a burst of energy, which could have only come from Dexter. He ran with all he had back to the mansion. Upon reaching the patio, exhaustion once again took over and he fell face down on the ground. Daniel squatted down in front of him.

"I see you met Maximus on your run," he said to Jonathan, who was still lying face down, fighting for the energy to stand up. With difficulty breathing and blurry vision, he looked up to see Reagan and the cheetah standing behind Daniel.

"Do I have to run again?" Jonathan asked, fearful of what the answer might be.

"No, not today," Daniel said, shaking his head. "On a normal day you'll be required to run ten miles, but not on your first day. Now get up and go change clothes. We need to get to the combat chamber." He turned and walked into the mansion with Maximus following behind. Reagan went over and squatted down in front of Jonathan. He was anxious to spend time in the combat chamber, but was still exhausted and, therefore, in no hurry to get up.

"That last part of your run was amazing," she told him. With that little bit of encouragement, and not wanting to look like a wimp in front of Reagan, he slowly began to pick himself up off the ground. Reagan helped him to his feet. He was anxious to get out of those heavy clothes and started to remove them. "Leave the clothes on and follow me," Reagan instructed.

"Reagan, these clothes weigh a ton, and now you're telling me I have to fight in them too?" he asked her.

"Yes," she replied. Putting all the weight on you now will benefit you later. I know who gave you the energy when you were running. How did you channel it? Dexter is dormant inside you so it's amazing how he can still help you at times." As they approached the door to the combat chamber they found Daniel impatiently waiting for them, arms crossed. The look on his face matched the tone of his voice.

"It's a good thing I wasn't dying here. That would have been a guaranteed death," he snapped. He held the door for Jonathan to come in. As he walked through the door, he could still hear Reagan talking.

"Good luck," she said. "Or break a leg, or however you say it." Amused by her attempt to use phrases well known to him, Jonathan turned to smile at her, but Daniel was already closing the door.

"Let's get started," Daniel said. "I'll set the level to the lowest possible." As soon as he started the chamber, a hologram appeared in front of Jonathan. Just as he saw it, the hologram charged him, sending Jonathan into the wall behind him. Reagan, who had been watching through a window, dropped her head in disgust. She could hardly stand seeing Jonathan be put through this. Keeping his mantra of not giving up, the teen got to his feet and threw a mighty punch at the hologram. The hologram dodged it, and came back at him with a hard blow to the chest, catching him by surprise, and once again sending him flying into the wall.

"That thing is killing him," cried Reagan, leaning up against the window.

"It is necessary for him to endure this to make him stronger," Daniel responded.

He pulled her away from the window.

"I know, but it's hard to watch this, especially..." Reagan started. Daniel cut her off in mid-sentence.

"When you love him?" Reagan turned and looked Daniel in the eyes.

"Yes, I do. And have for a long time now," she retorted. Daniel shook his head.

"There are a lot of unknowns about Jonathan," he said. In time we will talk about all of this." Having taken all he could take Daniel ended the session and opened the door. Reagan followed him into the chamber. Jonathan looked up at the two of them.

"This is going to hurt in the morning," he quipped. Not liking what she had witnessed during the session, Reagan ran to his side intent on helping him up. Seeing the stern look Daniel was giving her, she backed away from Jonathan. Unaware of the confrontation going on between his two hosts, Jonathan very gingerly picked himself up and got to his feet. "I hope the hot tub works really well," he said. "My body is going to pay dearly for this, I can feel it." Relieved to see Jonathan hadn't lost his good attitude, Daniel told him to go change clothes and meet them in the classroom.

"Reagan and I will meet you there. Don't take too long this time," Daniel reprimanded him. "We have a lot of things to discuss." Showing his eagerness to get in anything with a fast motor, Jonathan asked,

"What about the vehicle training? When will we get to that?"

"That will be last on the agenda," Daniel replied, shaking his head. Remembering he was just a teen, Daniel laughed, realizing that not even all this chaos could make a young man forget about fast cars. "Right now we have more important things to go over. Now go get out of those heavy clothes." They walked off, Jonathan going the opposite direction.

"Reagan, let me tell you this again." Daniel admonished her. "Do not pamper Jonathan or be so quick to run to his aid. Now let's get to the classroom."

"Daniel, I know what you keep telling me, but I can't help it. It's really hard," she pleaded. He shook his head.

"Remember, you also have powers that you have to keep under control. Being able to talk to animals will be very useful in his mission." When they got to the door to the classroom, Reagan scanned her retina to open the door for Daniel. "Go get the spa ready for Jonathan and then you may get lunch. Be sure to include a lot of proteins in his and make his plate larger than ours. I have a feeling he's going to have quite an appetite." She headed out the door, but not before getting one more reminder from Daniel. "Make sure you go directly to where you need to go and get done what you need to get done." Reagan hesitated, but without turning around or speaking, she walked out.

As the door closed behind her, Reagan saw Jonathan coming down the hall. His gait was very lethargic. When he got within reach, she put her hand on his chest.

"Are you okay?" she asked.

"Yeah, I'm okay," he replied. My entire body feels like jelly. Reagan, I hope I can do this. I did not know what to expect, but so far I'm not doing so well. I found the power to run the last part of the mile this morning, but that really wasn't me. And even with that, what good is it if I get my butt kicked by a low level hologram!" he worried.

"Give it time," Reagan reassured him. "Everything will fall into place. I'm sure of it." As she started to walk away, she turned back and added, "When you're finished in the classroom, come on back to the Jacuzzi in the back of the house. It will be ready for you."

"Oh, I'll be there as soon as I can," he replied. My body is screaming to get in there." He opened the door and just as he expected, Daniel was waiting there for him.

"Have a seat, Jonathan," he began. "Let's talk about Dexter, you and your family. If you're up to it, I'd like to start with the night your house blew up." Jonathan dropped his head.

"Not up to it at all and don't think I'll ever be. But if we need to talk about it, then let's do it."

"Thanks. I know it's hard," Daniel started. "You went out that night. To the movies, I believe. What was the name of the girl?"

"Krista," Jonathan answered.

"Right. Okay you and Krista went out. Where exactly did the two of you go?"

"We went to the movies and then she took me to a psychic's house. She said it would be fun to have our palms read. The lady told me about a power living inside me and that I should go home quickly because my family was in danger."

"Let's talk about Krista for a minute. What was her reaction to all of this? You came out of the room in a panic, is that right? Was Krista concerned at all?" Jonathan paused for a moment, thinking back on that night.

"I don't remember her being all that concerned, now that you mention it. She wasn't frightened when we were in the car. She told me to take her car and go if I needed to. I thought that was strange. Why would she want me to leave her out in the country? I told her no, to get in the car, but that I would drive. Do you think she had something to do with this?"

"No, I'm just saying that you have to look at all the facts. I agree with you, about why she would suggest that you leave her there. It's just as easy for her to drop you off at your house."

"For some strange reason, what you're asking about Krista wouldn't surprise me." "What happened once you got in the house?" Daniel asked.

"When we got to the house it was dark. I ran inside screaming for my Mom and sister. I heard a man's voice coming from upstairs. He was groaning. I ran in my Mother's room and found them all lying on the floor. The man I heard was only lying a few feet away from them. I yelled and screamed but they couldn't hear me. I went to the man and started shaking him, demanding to know who did this. He told me that my family had been poisoned and that there was a bomb in the basement and for me to hurry up and get out." Jonathan hung his head and wanted to cry. "Now here I am training with you to save the day, and I couldn't even save my own family."

"Don't beat yourself up, son," Daniel said. "There's nothing you could have done. But there is something for you to do now, and its best done without your anger or self-pity. The mission will be more likely to succeed if you have a pure heart. I know you want answers and revenge, but seeking revenge could be your downfall. And a pure heart will help establish you in Dexter's powers." Jonathan nodded his head, understanding what Daniel was saying. He needed to focus all his thoughts and energy on the mission itself. If the mission was a success then revenge would surely follow. Daniel continued, "Speaking of Dexter, Jonathan, you need to let whatever power comes through from him help you to focus. Don't fight the power when you feel it. Learn to embrace it. Even though he is dormant, Dexter's powers can be of great assistance to you. You've already experienced it, this morning when you were running."

"I'm not trying to change the subject," Jonathan interjected. "I don't understand the holograms. How am I supposed to get a direct hit? They move so fast, and I've only seen them at their slowest. How can I ever be ready for this?"

"Jonathan, that goes back to what I was saying about focusing all the power and energy that you get from Dexter. Not only do you need to have a pure heart, you also need to have a clear conscience. Never fight angry. It impedes your focus and blocks the flow of power between the two of you. Remember, Dexter can still give you power even though he's dormant. This was only your first day. There are techniques that you will learn. Don't let yourself get discouraged. There's still so much you have to learn. Your mind will become clearer as you learn everything."

"What are these techniques you mentioned? Something I've never seen before? Do I use the weapons with them?" Jonathan had many questions. Daniel shook his head.

"We won't get into that today. You really won't need them until after you return from the cave. Believe me, you'll be impressed with some of these techniques. But always remember, and I can't say it enough, it all hinges on your attitude. You have got to focus and be able to put your sorrow, anger and doubts aside. Most importantly, you have to be willing to put all this aside. For the good of the mission and the world."

"But sir, what if I fail?" Jonathan asked, with uncertainty in his voice.

"Jonathan, I truly believe that you won't. I have every faith in you. We all do. Remember I told you we had a lot to discuss in this classroom? The main focus of these sessions is to talk things out, answer as many of your questions and concerns as we can. This will help encourage you and aid in your mental preparation. With Dexter awake, communication would be so easy between the two of you. Until that time you have to know how to channel the vague signals that you're getting from him."

"Are you saying this is sort of like Morse code?" Jonathan asked. Daniel chuckled.

"Yes, I guess in a way, you could say that it is." As they were talking Jonathan's necklace began to light up. "The way it's blinking indicates that Dexter is restless. Like he's tossing and turning. It won't be long before he wakes up. We need to concentrate on your training. You need to head to the spa. After that I'm sure you'll be ready for lunch."

"Daniel," Jonathan began. "You know I'm consumed with anger and revenge. I promise you I will put all that aside and do my best in the training and the mission. I want to be prepared and win this battle. For my family."

"All you need is thirty minutes to soak, be sure and set the timer. I'll see you at lunch", said Daniel. He smiled and left the room. Jonathan sat there thinking. Looking down at the necklace, he noticed it was blinking in a different pattern than before. His thoughts became words.

"Dmitri must be out there somewhere. Whenever we meet, Dmitri, or whoever you are…I will take you down." He stood up and headed for the door. While crossing the room, he looked up to see Maximus standing there, staring at him. He slowly walked up to Jonathan. "How did you get in here?" Jonathan asked. Without uttering a word, the cheetah turned and exited the room, walking through the wall. Jonathan's eyes grew wide. Shaking his head and walking out the door he said, "This place gets weirder and weirder by the minute."

Chapter Nine

Jonathan got to the spa, and the hot tub looked so inviting. He could tell it was hot by the steam rising above it. He quickly stripped down to his boxers. Remembering the last shower he had where the water was hot but not scalding him, he jumped into the water. Jumping out faster than he got in, he was hopping around in circles, screaming.

"Hot! Man, that water is hot!" He was unaware that Reagan was in the shadows quietly watching. She was afraid she wouldn't be able to keep her laughing quiet. She wasn't ready to let him know she was there. She watched as Jonathan set the timer and eased himself cautiously into the hot tub. Maximus walked up and joined her. Without taking her eyes off of Jonathan she spoke.

"What do you think of him?" she asked the cheetah. Maximus studied Reagan for a moment, then turned his attention back to the spa.

"I can feel his power, yet there is something else about him that strikes me. Something else that makes him special." He paused before continuing. "Reagan I can see that your love for him has grown deeper since his arrival at the mansion."

"I can't help it," Reagan exclaimed. "Daniel keeps warning me to leave him alone, but it's hard." Glancing down at Maximus she asked, "How are things looking in the future?"

"We can't begin training Tomen until we hear the great roar of the Supremacy Dragon," he replied. The Newmanians are headed to our planet to launch their invasion. But, my dear, that's light years away." His attention shifted back to the young man in the hot tub. "I'm concerned, Reagan, for I sense a greater power within the boy than only Dexter. As though there is a hidden secret within his heart waiting to be unlocked."

The cheetah turned and left the spa. Seizing this opportunity to talk to Jonathan, Reagan walked to the hot tub. She was wearing a bikini bottom and a tee shirt, and had a towel wrapped around her waist. She sat on the edge and put her feet in the water. Thinking he was alone, this startled Jonathan and he sat up and was happy to see her sitting there.

"How long did Daniel say for you to soak?" she asked. He came up out of the water and sat beside her.

"Thirty minutes," Jonathan replied. "Where did you come from? I didn't hear you come in."

"I was hiding in the shadows, watching you," she laughed. His face turned a deep red. She saw that he was embarrassed.

"Did you see everything?" he wondered. He dropped his head and began to laugh at himself.

"Yes, I saw everything," she replied. At the same time they both looked at the timer, which read nineteen minutes. Jonathan slipped back down into the water. He wanted to remain seated next to Reagan, but with sore muscles, he didn't want to lose any time in the hot tub.

"The strangest thing happened just as I was leaving the classroom," he told her.

"Daniel had already left and I was about to, all of a sudden Maximus was standing there staring at me. I asked how he got in there, I thought you and I were the only ones with access. He didn't say anything, just turned and walked through the wall! I've never seen anything like it!"

"Maximus is a cheetah from the future. He's from your planet, but from one thousand years from now. He is here to help you," Reagan explained. "He is part of nature's defenders from that era. Things are different then from what you know now. People are the same, but the animals have more of a purpose. They serve to protect the earth's existence. There is someone just like you waiting to be trained by the animals."

Jonathan looked at her questioningly. This all sounded farfetched but that didn't diminish his curiosity. Reagan continued, "That's not anything for us to worry about right now. Our only mission here is to defeat Dmitri."

"I'm well aware of that," Jonathan snapped. Reagan could tell he was irritated at being told that continually. They sat there for a minute, Jonathan glaring at Reagan. They both suddenly realized the timer was going off.

"We'd better get out of here and go eat," Reagan said, standing up. As they got out of the hot tub, Jonathan grabbed her, pulled her in close and kissed her. Reagan started to pull away, but felt so comfortable wrapped in his arms that she allowed herself to enjoy this moment. She wasn't even aware that he had gotten her wet. Jonathan gently ended the kiss and reached for a towel off the table.

"Come on," Jonathan pleaded. "I'm starving. And if we don't get there soon, Daniel's likely to have an aneurism."

"Yeah, you're right," she replied, biting her bottom lip. She hated to see the moment end, especially not knowing when they would have another chance. As he walked to the door she watched drops of water run down the back of his neck. Jonathan turned around when she grabbed the towel from around his shoulders. More than anything Reagan wanted him to kiss her again. She tried to make it happen, but Jonathan put his hand between their lips. In heated frustration, she smirked, "You'll give me what I want sooner or later. Now turn around so I can dry off your back." Jonathan did as she commanded and turned around.

"Do you mind if I ask you a personal question, Reagan? How long has it been since you've been with a man?" The question surprised her, she couldn't be sure what he was thinking, why he was asking.

"I'm just like you," she replied. Seeing the look of surprise on his face, she hit him in the back of the head with the towel. "Yes, I'm a virgin." She pushed him playfully, causing him to stumble forward. "Now hurry up, we only have a few minutes to get to the kitchen." They hurried into the room and didn't know what to think when Daniel wasn't there. The two of them fixed themselves a plate and began eating. The conversation remained about Daniel and where he may have run off to.

"Did he say anything to you about going anywhere before he left the classroom? " Reagan asked.

"No," Jonathan replied. "Just that he was going to his room for a minute before heading to the kitchen." Not long after they sat down, in strolled Daniel. He fixed his plate and joined them at the table. Reagan was the first to speak.

"Where did you go?" she asked him.

"I went back to where Jonathan's house was and talked to some of the neighbors about that night. A house exploded; surely someone saw something." He glanced up at both of them. "Everything alright here, I assume?" he asked.

"Yes," they exclaimed in unison. Daniel looked bewildered but knew there was something he didn't want to hear about. He would deal with it later, as need be. Reagan wanted to change the subject, but Jonathan beat her to it.

"So what did you find out about that night?" he asked. Daniel hesitated.

"Two of the neighbors said that they heard you pull up, and shout to Krista as you went into the house. Your shouting is what made them look outside. When she pulled away from the house, she didn't drive off. She drove a couple of houses down, parked on the side of the road and turned her lights off. The lady across the street watched the car, wondering what was going on. It was only a couple of minutes later that your house exploded. The neighbor stood in shock, but noticed that the car drove past her and sped away." Jonathan's eyes began to tear up.

"You think Krista had something to do with this, don't you?" Out of Daniel's sight, Reagan reached under the table and put her hand on Jonathan's knee and softly rubbed it. She wanted to help him calm down. Daniel didn't respond. "Please

Daniel, tell me! That's what you think, isn't it?" Jonathan
begged getting up from the table. "I can't believe this at all!"

"Yes, son. I believe that she did. You need to calm
down, Jonathan. I think Katherine and Caroline were just
victims caught in the crossfire. The reason for the explosion
still puzzles me, though." Jonathan was no longer hearing
anything being said. He left the room and sprinted upstairs.
Daniel kept talking, but now to Reagan. "There is so much
more that ties in with what we already know to be happening.
Reagan, I want you to keep close to Jonathan. Make sure he
doesn't lose control. He needs to come to terms with all of this
so he can keep focused on the mission. And I'll say it one more
time, please keep your hands to yourself!" She heard every
word he said, but was elated to know she was instructed to stay
close to Jonathan. She stopped herself from smiling.

"Why do you think she's involved, Daniel?" Reagan
asked.

"Whenever this training is over and the two of you
return to school, you're going to have to keep a very close eye
on the both of them. There's still a lot that we don't know."
Daniel kept glancing toward the door, wondering if Jonathan
would come back.

"I just can't wrap my mind around the meaning of the house.
The family was dead. Why take out the house? Certainly not

the best way to do things quietly." Once again he turned his attention to Reagan. "As all of this unfolds, make sure you stay out of harm's way," he told her.

"What makes you say that?" asked Reagan. She was a little dismayed.

"Just pointing out that Dmitri will stop at nothing to get anybody that's tied in with Jonathan. I'm hoping your feelings for him don't keep you from seeing danger when it shows up."

"Doesn't everybody think Jonathan is dead?" she asked. Nodding his head, Daniel responded.

"Yes, that's true, for now. When the time comes and he's back out there, everybody will see that he's alive. Don't you figure that will be quite a shock to the world?" Reagan nodded, and thought for a moment before she spoke.

"You told me to go talk to the neighbors to see what I could find out from them about that night. What made you decide to go yourself? And why did you go without letting anyone know where you were? Daniel, what are you hiding?" she demanded to know.

"I'm not hiding anything," he said. "I had a sudden urge to go see for myself what I could find out. I had some time while Jonathan was in the spa."

"You're hiding something, I know you are. I can see a fire in your eyes. What is it that you won't tell us? Daniel, I've known you a long time and I know when you're fired up about something. What is it about Jonathan being the one that has you so worked up?" Daniel got up from the table and headed to put his dishes in the sink.

"I'm not hiding anything from anyone," he said again. "I wanted to find out for Jonathan." Reagan followed him with her own dishes.

"You're hiding something," she muttered under her breath, but still meant to be heard.

"Fine," Daniel whispered, exasperated. Aloud he said, "If you must know, come back to the table and have a seat." When they both were seated at the table, he told her the story. "Years ago when I was a detective, before the keepers of the gate recruited me for this mission, I was thought to be assisting the FBI with a drug raid. When I reached the drugs I was suddenly thrown about a hundred feet into the air, but I never came down. Just like Jonathan, I ended up here. They changed my looks and gave me a new name." Reagan sat quietly, waiting for him to go on. When he didn't, she thought back on their previous conversation. She realized there was more to the story than she could imagine.

"Wait a minute," she said. "Jonathan's more important to you than you've been letting on. What are you trying to say Daniel?"

"Reagan, Jonathan is my son." Reagan expected a bomb to drop, but this wasn't the news she expected. She would never have guessed this was the secret he'd been hiding. Her face dropped.

"Are you going to tell him? Don't you think he deserves to know?" she asked.

"That's not a very good idea and now is definitely not the appropriate time to do so," Daniel responded, shaking his head.

"That's not right, Daniel," Reagan exclaimed. He's always missed you not being around and right now he's feeling abandoned and alone. He needs to know that he still has family and that someone is on his side."

"Reagan, don't you think this is hard for me? He's my son! I had to leave my wife and young children and now they're dead. The fate of the world is in the hands of my son. I have to prepare him for battle against forces he's never seen the likes of. And worst of all, I have to SEND him into battle. You don't think that's hard? You don't think I want to tell him who I am? He has enough to deal with right now, this would only add to the list of distractions right now." Reagan shook her head. She still didn't think this was a good idea.

"Please, Daniel, considering everything Jonathan's been through, this would be the perfect time to tell him. He needs hope. He thinks he's lost his entire family and it's not true! Did you know that I have pictures of Katherine and Caroline on the day they died?" She looked over his shoulder, staring into space. "We were just playing around that afternoon. Now those are the last pictures of them. The last of his family." She looked at Daniel, shook her head and headed for the door.

"Reagan, keep this between us!" he pleaded.

Chapter Ten

Everyone gathered for the meeting. There were eighteen of them before Dmitri entered the room. As he made his entrance everyone stood up.

"You may all be seated," he said as he made his way to the head of the table. He remained standing, gazing one by one at everyone seated around the table. "I want to compliment Jason on a job well done," he said. "If anyone thinks as Kevin did, death will find them as well." He walked around the long table. His look was fierce and cold.

"Kevin felt the need to lie, steal and hide things from me. Jason, did you check my accounts?"

"All the money that Kevin took is back in the accounts," Jason stood and assured him.

"Did you also take care of the Bailey house? I hope there was no evidence left behind." Jason nodded.

"The Bailey house was destroyed, taking with it any and all evidence." Jason was Dmitri's right hand man. He had been given a small portion of Dmitri's powers, which made him look younger than his twenty five years. Although the portion was small, they made Jason more powerful than any human. They also made him fast, strong and very cunning. Jason stood 6'3" tall and was a muscular young man. Dmitri's forces were led by Jason.

"Now, is there anyone that can link your team to this crime?" Dmitri asked, walking back to the head of the table.

"No, sir," Jason replied. Before Jason could say anymore, the door opened and Krista entered the room.

"There may be one," she said, joining the meeting. She sat down on the left side of Dmitri.

"You did an excellent job," he told her. "Now, what were you saying?"

"The palm reader that I took Jonathan to. She lives in Lakeview. There's no telling what all she may know."

"Jason, at the conclusion of this meeting I want you to find this psychic's house and bring her to me," Dmitri ordered. As he spoke, the necklace around his neck began to blink. He looked down at it and said, "My brother, Dexter, will soon be revived. We must finish digging and find that golden box and destroy it. If Dexter awakens, the box will automatically open and the Supremacy Dragon will be under his control. Now that the house is gone we can bring the fortress to the surface. There is enough uranium underneath that block to run all of our transports. And I'm the only one who knows that my father hid the golden box under the Bailey house. So you see why this is so important. We must find that box and destroy it." He turned to his left. "Krista, are you absolutely positive that Jonathan ran into the house just before it exploded?"

"Yes, definitely," she reassured him. "I watched him run into the house. Then I turned my lights off and parked a few houses down so I could watch the explosion and make sure he didn't come out." Dmitri's attention turned back to the necklace.

"Whoever is hosting Dexter is trying to revive him. Our every move must be accurate and precise. This is what I want, Jason. Anyone who is friends or acquaintances of Jonathan's I want eliminated." Jason nodded in agreement. Krista spoke again.

"Jonathan had a friend, Charles, which he was close with. And there was a new girl at school and they spent most of the day together."

"Everyone that is close to that family in any way, I want brought to me. Do you hear me, Jason?" Dmitri demanded.

"The world will soon be ours. All the uranium we need is at our disposal. Once the golden box is destroyed, nothing can stop us. Jason, take your team and go ahead and take care of this Charles and the palm reader and find the new girl. And anyone you find that is connected to that family in the slightest, bring them to me." Jason, along with everyone else at the table got up without a word, and left. All except for Krista. She remained seated at the table. "Krista, did anyone see you drive off after the house exploded?" Dmitri wanted to know.

"No, I'm sure nobody did. I parked a few houses down. I didn't see anybody come out of their front doors." she answered.

"Good," Dmitri nodded with pleasure. "Keep an eye out at school. That guy who is supposed to be your boyfriend could become a problem."

"Michael is too distracted by sports and being a bully to notice anything happening right in front of him. That's why he's the perfect one to be my boyfriend. I'll keep a close eye on everything at school." Changing the subject, she asked him, "Just how powerful is Dexter?"

"Let me put it to you this way," Dmitri started. "With the power of the golden dragon, Dexter could destroy the earth with a snap of his fingers. With the golden box destroyed and the black dragon in my possession, no one can challenge me.

Not even the powerful Dexter. Krista, you've done an excellent job keeping an eye on Jonathan and his family for me all these years."

"When can I get out of school?" she asked him.

"Not yet. Stay there awhile longer until all this is finished and our reign is in motion. Please be patient and wait. You will see everything come full circle. I believe that what started at the house is not yet over. I have an uneasy feeling that Jonathan somehow may still be alive."

"So that's why you want me to stay at the school longer, isn't it?" Krista asked him.

"Yes, it is," he answered. "If he's still alive, you should be the first of our team to find out as he'll most likely show back up at school. I need you to keep your eyes open for anything." Krista nodded and left the room.

Dmitri walked around the table and removed his phone from his pocket. It wasn't long before Jason answered. "We're moving the site to underneath the house. Is everything fully operational?" he asked. The news must have been pleasing. Dmitri smiled as he hung up the phone, poured himself a drink and sat down. The anger towards his brother that he let everybody see was actually fear. Dexter was the one person he was afraid of. His thoughts turned into words as the necklace began blinking once again.

"Dexter I know you're out there, but you're not awake yet. I'm close to finding that box and when I do, you and the box will be destroyed. I should have killed you when I killed our father all those years ago." He studied the blueprints of the block, finished his drink and left.

Chapter Eleven

Jonathan came downstairs to head outside for his speed and conditioning session. He was one month into his training. Surprised to find himself alone on the patio, wondering where Daniel and Reagan were, he hollered out for Maximus. He was determined to train to the best of his abilities no matter what.

"Maximus, where are you?" he shouted. The cheetah appeared from out of the bushes. "I'm ready to run," Jonathan said with enthusiasm in his voice. He knelt down into a starting position and yelled, "Go!" They both took off running and Jonathan was staying close to the cheetah, but was well aware that Maximus was holding back. Jonathan could no longer feel the heavy weight of the suit he wore and was running faster than was humanly possible. Maximus let Jonathan take the lead for a few seconds, and then went flying by the young man. Maximus allowed him to catch up to him without letting him retake the lead, and they returned to the patio at the same time.

"You have done well, Jonathan," he heard Daniel say. Reagan stood behind Daniel, clapping softly. Checking his stopwatch he continued, "You ran the mile in two minutes that time. You're improving nicely. And I see that Maximus had to use the power sooner this time, in order to keep you from passing him." Daniel grinned at the cheetah.

"What did you do different this time?" Reagan asked Jonathan. He shrugged his shoulders.

"I don't know. Dexter, I guess."

"You're really coming along in your training, Jonathan," Daniel said. "Time to step it up a notch, I think. Tomorrow you and I will go to the Aqueous Cave and retrieve the swords and medallion. Also, the cave will reveal things about you that only I will be able to see."

"Sounds interesting," Jonathan remarked. By now he was used to there being weird stuff popping up here and there. Jonathan walked over to Maximus and patted him on the head. "Good workout today," he thanked him.

The feelings between Jonathan and Reagan had grown since he first came to the mansion. He was too busy training to really notice that nothing was happening between the two, but the feelings were there. He gave her a glance as he stood to follow Daniel. She returned his look with a casual smile.

"Good job today," Daniel said, to no one in particular. "Are you ready for the combat chamber?" As they walked inside Daniel kept talking to Jonathan. "I'm proud of how well your training is progressing. Are you ready for something new? I think we'll raise the level today in the chamber." He headed for the control panel while Jonathan entered the chamber.

"Wish me luck," Jonathan requested.

"I always do," replied Reagan. Making sure not to be seen by Daniel, she lightly ran her hand down Jonathan's cheek.

"Are you ready?" Daniel asked.

"Ready when you are," came the reply. Jonathan quickly gave Reagan a wink before giving all his attention to the session. Clenching his fists in anticipation, he wondered where the first hologram would appear. He no sooner had the thought when the first one appeared and threw a hard jab. Jonathan was ready for them today and ducked to avoid getting hit. Suddenly the other nine holograms appeared and began to attack. Seeing that he was pretty much able to hold his own, Reagan commented.

"My God, Daniel. He's gotten so much faster. He's so much more agile. He's dodging their punches." As they watched three of the holograms surround Jonathan, they were amazed to see him kneel down and trip all of them with his leg. As the next one came at him full force, Jonathan jumped and found himself fourteen feet in the air, coming down on top of it so hard that it exploded. Daniel and Reagan looked on in awe. His hands were moving so fast, they could barely see them. As the fighting continued, Jonathan hit the next four so hard they also exploded. The remaining five holograms all started running in a circle around him. They were moving at such a high speed that they were creating winds like the young man had never experienced before. Reagan and Daniel turned to look at each other.

"Let's see how he deals with this turn of events," Daniel said. He was anxious to see Jonathan's response, but Reagan couldn't watch and turned her head. She also crossed as many fingers as she could. Jonathan squatted down in a stance that even Daniel had never before seen. "What on earth is he doing?" Daniel asked out loud. Her curiosity peaked, Reagan turned around to see what Daniel was talking about. Jonathan stood straight up and was clenching both hands in front of him, as if he were mustering up all the energy he had. Stretching out his arms with open hands, he spoke simply.

"Smoke screen." Smoke filled the chamber as the holograms charged at Jonathan. Once again afraid to watch, fearing the worst, Reagan turned her head. She could tell that Daniel excitement was growing.

"This is amazing," she heard him say. She turned back to look through the window to see the chamber so full of smoke that they could no longer see anything except holograms one by one being thrown against the glass. When the last of them hit the glass and exploded, the smoke cleared and there stood Jonathan. In the same stance they had seen before the smoke, he stood like stone, not moving except for his chest as he took each breath.

Forgetting that Daniel was standing beside her, Reagan let her excitement for Jonathan overcome her, and she opened the door to the chamber, ran in and threw her arms around him.

"Where did that come from?" she asked him. Not wanting to irritate Daniel, Jonathan didn't respond. He whispered to Reagan.

"Did you forget who you were standing with out there?" She slowly lowered her arms to her sides and expected Daniel to start giving her lip about her and Jonathan. Hearing nothing from him at all, she glanced up at Jonathan, trying to get an idea what was happening behind her. Jonathan kept his eyes on Daniel, and suggested that Reagan exit the chamber first. Following close behind her, he noticed that Daniel was just staring, as if in a trance. Assuming he was upset with the two of them, Jonathan quickly wanted to change the subject, so to speak.

"So, sir. What did you think?" he asked. Daniel didn't come out of his trance for a couple of seconds, and finally answered.

"Son, that was incredible," he exclaimed, crossing his arms. The holograms were moving so fast, but your arms were moving even faster. When you took your stance, I couldn't wait to see what you had up your sleeve, but then the smoke screen appeared. It was outstanding when they started flying out of the smoke. I really wanted to be able to see what you were doing. I know it was extraordinary. How on earth did you think to do that?" Daniel asked.

"I can't explain it," Jonathan replied, shaking his head. "As I stood there it just came to me automatically." He turned and started walking towards the door. "I'm going to go clean up and change. Daniel, I'll meet you in the classroom when I'm done."

"Jonathan is very powerful," Daniel said, as he turned to Reagan. "Maximus said the same thing. That there is something different about Jonathan." Reagan noticed Daniel pause and that the look on his face changed. She hoped he wasn't going to ask about the one thing she didn't want to talk about. "So, what's going on with you and Jonathan?" he asked her. Reagan dropped her head. That was it. The one thing she didn't want to talk about.

"What do you mean?" she asked, innocently.

"Reagan, I can see that your relationship with Jonathan has grown since he's been here. At the end of the session I barely had time to move before the door was open and you were wrapped around him. So I'm asking again, what is up with you two?"

"How can you ask me that when you're hiding the fact that you're his father?" she accused him. "Yes, he's come a long way, but there are still nights that he has trouble sleeping and I've held him because of his fears. The longer you wait to tell him, it's going to be more painful for you in the long run."

"I will tell him in due time," Daniel told her. They heard Jonathan coming back downstairs, so their conversation was over. The young man was surprised to see them.

"I thought you'd already be in the classroom," he said to Daniel.

"Reagan, why don't you go ahead and fix lunch?" Daniel turned to face Reagan and gave her a stern look that Jonathan couldn't see. Turning back to Jonathan, he told him, "There won't be a classroom session today. You've done really well with your training but tomorrow we go to the cave and you're going to need to rest. Go ahead and take the rest of the day for yourself. Relax, but try to stay levelheaded."

"How am I supposed to do that?" Jonathan asked.

"Relax, rest and just keep your mind at peace," replied Daniel. Not another word was said as he watched Jonathan trot off to the kitchen, no doubt in search of Reagan. Daniel dropped his head and walked off.

As Jonathan reached the kitchen he saw that Reagan had her back to the door. He snuck up behind her and yelled.

"AHHHHHHH!" Screaming at the top of her lungs, Reagan turned around, both arms swinging. Jonathan was laughing hard but managed to dodge her fists.

"That wasn't fair, Jonathan," she scolded him. He finally quit laughing, pulled her in close and kissed her.

"What were you thinking busting into the chamber like that?" he demanded to know.

"I don't know," she said, shrugging her shoulders. She wrapped her arm around his neck. "I was just so proud of you. I couldn't watch some of it, but you were great at the end. I was relieved that you were okay. I forgot all about Daniel standing there." They started kissing again when Reagan pulled away. "I need to get lunch ready, so if you'll kindly stop distracting me," she said with a grin. Jonathan jumped up and sat on the countertop next to where she was cooking. She was frying fish and tossing a green salad. "It made me nervous watching you today. Especially when the holograms started surrounding you." He nearly interrupted her.

"I don't want to talk about anything to do with training. I have a free afternoon." He slid off the counter and walked up behind her. Turning her around to face him, Jonathan took both of her hands in his. "You've been a big help to me, Reagan," he said softly. "Any talk of fighting I'll do with Daniel. When I'm with you all I want to talk about is us and fun things."

"You know Daniel thinks I'm distracting you, don't you?" she asked him. She turned back to the fish. "You've been around him long enough to know how he is."

"So what is he talking about? Look how things are turning out," said Jonathan.

"My training is going great. I'm so comfortable when I'm with Daniel. We get along great."

"Yeah, I wonder why?" she mumbled under her breath. Jonathan looked at her.

"What did you say?" he asked.

"Nothing," she quickly replied. "Tonight before you go to bed, we'll look at the pictures of your family on my phone again, if you'd like."

"That's fine, Reagan. As long as I'm spending time with you."

"Remember, we have to contain ourselves for the sake of this mission," she warned him.

"Look who's talking about abstinence," Jonathan said grinning. He walked to the table and sat down. He watched as she moved around the kitchen preparing lunch. Reagan was well aware that his eyes were on her. She smiled to herself. She began singing softly and swaying to her own voice. She managed to steal a couple of glances in his direction. This was a side of her Jonathan had never seen.

"What a beautiful voice. I didn't know you could sing." Her voice reminded him of his mother and when she would sing as she did things around the house. His heart melted. After watching her for a while longer he joined her in the kitchen. He walked up behind her and put his hands on her shoulders. "I love hearing you sing, Reagan." Lost in their feelings for each other neither one of them heard Daniel enter the kitchen.

"I know you're cooking lunch, but I have to go out again," Daniel said to Reagan. Both she and Jonathan froze.

"Is this pertaining to what we were talking about earlier?" she asked him.

"No," he replied. "I need to pick up some things for the house." Without another word Daniel went to the garage. Jonathan removed his hands from Reagan's shoulders and sat back down at the table. She brought the food and sat down across the table from him and they began to eat. Knowing how he felt and not sure what would become of them, Jonathan lost his appetite and left the table, barely touching his lunch. He had a strong feeling that Reagan was playing cat and mouse with him. As soon as he got to the stairs he sprinted to the top. Expecting that she couldn't resist following him, Jonathan hid behind the door waiting. Sure enough, he heard footsteps sprinting up the stairs just as he had done. Not realizing that he was behind the door, Reagan stopped when she entered the room and wondered where he had gone. Coming from behind her, Jonathan grabbed her, spun her around and kissed her. This time more passionately than he had before. Both of them feeling like there was nothing to stop them, they let their hands run freely and they began undressing each other. Reagan reached over his shoulder and pushed the door closed.

Chapter Twelve

Daniel walked out the front door and sat down. Maximus came walking up and stood beside him.

"What's on your mind, Daniel?" the cheetah asked his friend. Daniel shook his head and sighed.

"Everything about today," he said. "Mainly those two young people in the house."

"I take it you haven't told him that you're his father," Maximus questioned. Again, Daniel shook his head.

"I just don't think it's a good idea, Maximus. What good would come of it?"

"Daniel, this is none of my business, but you need to think long and hard on all the good that could come from him knowing. The boy has lost everyone in his family. Everyone that he loves. He needs to know that not only does he have family still alive, but they are here pulling for him."

"My son already thinks I'm dead, and has for a lot of years. How do you think he'll take it all of a sudden finding out that I'm alive? I don't even look like I did back then, like he remembers me." Maximus sat down and looked at Daniel.

"He's gotten to know you this past month, Daniel. If you don't tell him now, how do you expect him to understand hearing about it later? You have to be honest with him and don't leave out any of the details. Be specific, especially when answering his questions. And I'm sure there will be many." The cheetah looked off in the distance and continued, as if speaking to no one in particular. "The boy has extraordinary power. I've been watching him and I truly believe that he will save the world. It would give him hope and help him in his mission to know that all is not lost." They both stood up and headed out the trail, this time walking instead of the high speeds this trail was used for daily.

"You should have seen him in the chamber today, Maximus," Daniel remarked, the excitement evident in his voice. "He was phenomenal. Tomorrow we'll go to the cave and he'll retrieve the medallion and swords. What's mysterious about today were the moves he was using. They came from Jonathan himself. Not anything like Dexter has ever done."

"Just as I thought. I've been watching the boy and there is definitely something different about him. I see it every time I watch him train. When we ran this morning his speed grew quickly," said Maximus. "How do you think he'll do in the cave tomorrow?"

"I believe he'll obtain everything he needs to. After he gets the swords the medallion will automatically come to him."

"That's what you're most afraid of, isn't it?" Maximus asked. He stopped and looked at his friend.

"It sure doesn't help being his father. Sending him into that cave knowing how easily he could lose his life, and I could lose my son," Daniel said wearily.

"He'll be fine," the cheetah reassured him. "Look at all that's been accomplished in just a month. He's done well since he's been here. Remember, he still has four more months of training to go. Try to think positively." They started walking again.

"The cave is hot and dense," Daniel said. "But I believe his power will sustain him while he's inside. He still must move swiftly." They stepped onto the patio.

"Where is Jonathan now?" Maximus wondered, looking around. Daniel crossed his arms and nodded towards the house.

"He's inside with Reagan," he answered.

"How are you handling that situation?" Daniel's head dropped.

"The more I try to keep them apart just seems to drive them together." Maximus laughed and shook his head.

"It is destined for those two to be together, Daniel. It is written in the scrolls, so you should do your best to accept it and let it be."

"I'm his father. He's only eighteen and she's thirty eight. How can I just let that be?"

"I know it's hard," agreed Maximus. "But you know Reagan's not just any woman. In a sense, she's almost like your daughter."

Feeling a bit more relaxed Daniel admitted, "Speaking in terms of the age difference, that's all. He's my son and I know she's been like a daughter. They're always together in the house. Acting like a young couple in love. It's hard to watch when they can't keep their hands off of each other."

"And how are you dealing with the deaths of Katherine and Caroline?" was Maximus' next question. Daniel paused and gazed up towards the sky.

"It's almost more than I can bear, my friend. Not only knowing they were in the house when it exploded, but they were murdered before that. I've missed them so much, and now this. It's driving me mad, but it's also what's driving me more than anything to succeed in this mission."

"Daniel," Maximus pressured him. "Then you should do what is right and tell Jonathan that his father is alive and that you are him. That would make this training mean more to both of you as well."

"I don't know, Maximus," Daniel responded, shaking his head. "I know that he misses his family and it's hard for me to tell him to try and put that sorrow aside and focus on the mission. I know what he's feeling, because I miss them too!" He hesitated and looked at Maximus. "And now Reagan also knows."

"When did you tell her?" he asked.

"The other day when we were talking. She could tell I was hiding something. She kept badgering me about it, so I told her."

"Do you think that was a good idea? Especially as close as they've become of late," the cheetah said.

"Reagan gave me her word that she wouldn't tell him. She agrees with you, that Jonathan should know. But I think she knows it's something that my son should hear from me."

Suddenly they heard laughter coming from inside the house. Both man and cheetah turned to see the kids running around the dining room table. Jonathan was chasing Reagan, apparently trying to get his shirt from her. Daniel turned back to Maximus.

"Do you see what I mean?" he asked. "She's thirty eight years old and look how she carries on."

"Daniel, do you remember being that young and your first love?" Maximus asked him. "Yes, she's thirty years old, but she never really had a childhood, a first crush or any of that and those feelings don't just go away. It shouldn't surprise you, seeing as how they've been thrown together like this. Reagan's never experienced this so she's living it for the first time with Jonathan. She's sharing his feelings, his youth, and there's nothing wrong with that."

The young couple were still chasing each other inside. Jonathan noticed the two outside on the patio talking. He walked to the door, opened it and spoke to Daniel.

"I thought you were leaving."

"I changed my mind," was Daniel's reply. Reagan was still running around the room, oblivious to anyone at the mansion except for Jonathan. Seeing him at the door but not the two outside, she came closer and threw his shirt at him, hitting him in the head. Then she ran out of the room. Not sure what all Daniel had seen happen inside, Jonathan stood quietly with his shirt hanging from his head, waiting for Daniel to speak. Daniel grinned at him.

"You're not going to just stand there and let her get away with that, are you?"

Although surprised at Daniel's reaction, Jonathan grinned back, grabbed the shirt from his head and ran after Reagan.

"The only way you could keep those two apart is to kidnap one of them," Maximus said.

"So I see you're going to go ahead and let them be."

"You're right," he told the cheetah. I know I'm pushing Jonathan hard. Dmitri's out there and I'm angry. My family was murdered, the fate of the world is in the hands of my son, and I'm the one sending him out to do battle. I'm the one responsible for his training. Maximus, if this mission fails it will rest on my shoulders. If I could be the one to face Dmitri, I would."

"You'll be facing Dmitri all right. You'll be facing him through your son. I have every faith that you will bring Jonathan to his full potential and that Dexter will awaken."

Daniel took a seat at the edge of the patio. "Like I said earlier, there is something different about Jonathan. He already has more power than we expected. I believe there is more about your son than has been revealed yet, even to us." Maximus continued.

"Daniel, you've no doubt heard of the legend of the great wizard. It is rumored that he has hidden himself and will appear when the time is right."

"That's just legend," Daniel retorted. "This great wizard was killed by Dmitri. And any one killed by magic is dead, forever." There was silence on the patio. They were both deep in their own thoughts. After a few minutes their thoughts seemed to come together. Daniel looked quizzically at Maximus. "You don't think…you're not suggesting that Jonathan could be him, are you?"

"Daniel, think. You even said it yourself. Look at how your son moves in battle. We know that knowledge doesn't come from Dexter. The legend also talks about how Darius was before he created the two dragons. There was another dragon, a white one."

"I've heard that part of the legend too," said Daniel. "The white dragon of divinity. But that is just legend. Right now we have to get the golden dragon awake and time is running out. The only way for that to happen is for Jonathan to complete his training and be as prepared as he can be. We cannot concern ourselves with myths and legends. Tomorrow we will know whether or not we still have hope." They both looked towards the cave.

"I believe in the young man," said the cheetah. "And no matter what happens, I believe that he will save the world." Daniel stood up and headed inside.

"How can you be so sure?" Daniel asked him.

"The future depends on it."

"I know, my friend," replied Daniel. "I know." He went inside leaving Maximus standing alone on the patio. Daniel glanced up the stairs and smiled.

Chapter Thirteen

The mood was solemn when Daniel and Jonathan arrived at the Aqueous cave early that morning. Neither one of the men wanted to speak, afraid of what the other one might be thinking. Finally Daniel broke the silence.

"Jonathan, no matter what's happened in the past, today is the most important day of your life so far. You really have to focus on this. Block out everybody and everything that could be a distraction. Make no mistake, son, you will be in harm's way. And there's no turning back. You're totally on your own. No matter what happens inside the cave, I cannot help you in any way." Jonathan turned to face him.

"Don't worry, sir," Jonathan said. "I feel I can do this. Daniel, I just want to say thank you for everything you've done for me."

"I worry, but I know you can do this," Daniel assured him. "I need you to understand that you and only you can do this. I would help you if I could…" Jonathan interrupted.

"I know."

"Now, once inside the cave it will be hotter than you've ever experienced before. You must move as quickly as possible. According to the scrolls, as soon as you grab the swords, move to the circle and the medallion will appear before you. You will be able to grab it with no problem. Remember to move fast. If you fail in here, there's no coming back."

"I know," Jonathan repeated. This time he hung his head and sighed. "I will either grab the swords and medallion or I will die in the cave. I understand."

"You sound pretty confident," Daniel noticed.

"It's better than being a sourpuss, right sir?" Jonathan quipped. "Seriously, I know the gravity of the situation and today's the day. I'm either ready or I'm not, and I really feel that I am." Daniel nodded and they walked into the entrance to the cave. Looking in they were both amazed, especially Jonathan.

"These weapons were hidden in the past when Dmitri drowned Dexter," Daniel explained. Seeing that Jonathan never took his eyes off the inside of the cave, he reminded him,

"Remember, once you step inside you'll feel the immense heat. Do you see the sky?" Daniel asked. Jonathan looked up.

"Yes, I do," he replied. Daniel continued to explain.

"That sky will give me an indication of your power and the distinction between you and Dexter."

"What do you mean?" Jonathan asked.

"Just like in the combat chamber that day. There are techniques that are required that will not come from Dexter. They will come from within you. We refer to the technique as the "Dou Motion." If, no- *when*, you come out of the cave, you will also have earned two other techniques; the shield and neuron bomb. We will discuss these in class when you have earned them." Jonathan got a little boastful.

"*WHEN* I earn them is right", he said. Daniel gave him a look and smiled.

"The density of the air will not weigh you down until you reach the inner circle", Daniel continued. With a few more reminders the time had come. "Are you ready, son?" he asked.

"Yes," Jonathan replied and entered the cave standing outside the big circle.

"You were right about the heat. It's hot in here." Daniel nodded, and refrained from telling him it was two hundred and fifty degrees. That was just another distraction that was best avoided. Seeing how well Jonathan was dealing with the heat, Daniel got a good feeling about the chances of reviving Dexter. Jonathan was baring up well, but nevertheless, was pouring with sweat as if standing under running water. He took a deep breath and stepped into the circle. Immediately falling to his knees, the density was so high that it wasn't long before he was face down. Daniel watched with concern, glanced up at the sky to see only a small touch of gold in the clouds. He yelled, hoping he could be heard.

"Maybe this wasn't a good idea, Jonathan!" On the verge of losing consciousness, the young man heard nothing. His eyes closed as he felt as if he was taking his last few breaths. Daniel could only stand there helpless, looking in at his son's motionless body. He knew if he entered the cave it would be certain death for both of them. Tears began to trickle down Daniel's cheek after six minutes had passed. Still no motion from Jonathan. He frantically kept looking at the sky, but there was no change. The gold he could see was still very small. Daniel's heart was broken. He never told his son the truth about the two of them, and now he had sent him into this cave to his death. He grabbed his bag and headed out of the cave. Before he could reach the entrance, the cave began to shake violently. Unsure of what this meant, he turned and went back inside. There was Jonathan, standing tall with arms stretched out wide as smoke began to rise at his feet. "Jonathan, can you hear me?" he yelled.

"Yes," came the reply, but Daniel knew that wasn't Jonathan's voice. Not totally.

To him it almost sounded like a combination of two voices, and he knew that didn't make sense. He watched as Jonathan braved the heat and retrieved the swords that hung on the opposite wall of the cave. Daniel could see the sweat pouring off the young man's head and face and, trying to take in every detail, noticed that the boy's eyes were golden. They were so bright that it was almost blinding. Jonathan wearily made his way to the inner circle, holding on to his treasure. Standing up tall once again, he shouted, "Medallion," and the golden medallion appeared in front of him. Daniel was in awe and could barely believe what he was seeing. He had heard of this cave, taught for this very task, but still, there was nothing that compared to seeing it all take place. From where he was standing he could tell the temperature was rising inside. This was something he didn't expect, and he worried about the affect it would have on Jonathan. He looked to the sky and was relieved to see that about seventy five percent of it had a golden hue. Within the gold was a small round spot of white.

"Could what Maximus said about the legend really be true?" Daniel asked, thinking out loud. "Is it even possible?"

Jonathan was still making his way from the center of the cave towards Daniel.

His eyes still golden, Jonathan reached to opening of the cave and asked, "How did I do?" Before he could take another breath, he passed out, and Daniel caught him in his arms.

"You did fine, son. You did fine." Swelling with pride and relief Daniel picked Jonathan up and carried him back to the mansion. Jonathan was still clutching the medallion and swords.

Reagan had been pacing on the patio ever since they left for the cave. At the first sign of movement she strained to see if they were both coming back. She started to cry when she saw there was only one person walking. Strangely enough, though, she couldn't make out who it was. Still straining to see, she never blinked until she saw that Daniel was carrying Jonathan. Although she didn't know his condition she was still relieved that Daniel wasn't alone. As they neared the house, Reagan ran out to meet them. "What happened? Is he…?" she started to ask. They walked up to the patio, and

Daniel laid Jonathan down in a lounge chair.

"He's alive, but he had a rough time of it in there," Daniel replied. "Reagan, please go turn down his bed so I can take him up there."

"Do you want me to run a bath for him as well?" she asked.

"Yes, please. When he wakes up he will feel better than staying in those filthy clothes." Reagan jumped up from where she was kneeling beside Jonathan. By the time she got the bed turned down and the bath started she heard Daniel making his way upstairs, carrying Jonathan. He put him in the tub as it was filling up with water and left the room. Reagan could feel the tears welling up inside, no matter how hard she tried to hold them back. Moments later Daniel returned with a pair of scissors. "Here," he said, handing the scissors to Reagan. Cut his clothes off and get him cleaned up. Let me know when you're done and I'll take him to his room."

"Yes sir, I will," she responded. Daniel watched as she began cutting his clothes and noticed the tears she was trying to hold back.

Placing his hand on her shoulder, he said, "He's going to be fine, Reagan." She continued to dry her tears, and Daniel left and went downstairs. She looked back down at Jonathan and saw blood coming from his eyes. Quickly grabbing a washcloth she gently washed his face.

"I hope Daniel's right," she said aloud. As the water covered Jonathan's body, Reagan began to gently bathe him. Daniel walked back in.

"Jonathan did a fantastic job in the cave today," he boasted. Standing up to face Daniel, Reagan said,

"With all due respect, I don't think he did all that great. Look at him." Once again, she began to tear up.

"You look at him, Reagan. Put your feelings aside and look at him. He's alive, isn't he? We all knew that he would succeed inside the cave or die in there. He's here now so you know he didn't fail. And after what I saw him do today, I know the world has a better chance than I thought yesterday." She still had difficulty holding back her tears.

"What do you mean?" she asked. She knelt back down beside the tub and resumed bathing him.

"Jonathan is a very powerful young man in his own right. I can't explain it, but what we've been seeing from him isn't all coming from Dexter." Reagan could hear the pride in Daniel's voice. "I believe there's so much more we have to learn about him. It wasn't easy but he survived and completed the task inside the cave. Something neither one of us could have even attempted. The indication I got from the sky about the cave is that Dexter is very close to waking up. But we're running out of time. You and Jonathan will have to return to earth and resume your roles as high school students." She was just about finished bathing Jonathan. Daniel continued. "When you return to school it will only have been five of their days that you've been gone. We are at a race against time from this point on." As he carried Jonathan to the bedroom and put him in bed, they saw that his necklace began to light up and blink. "Like I said, we have to move quickly. Dmitri's necklace should be blinking just as this one is, so he surely knows that the time is coming when Dexter will be revived." Reagan looked perplexed.

"So you're telling me that Dmitri has a necklace as well?" she asked.

"Yes, he does," Daniel went on to explain. "His necklace works the same as Jonathan's. However, the black dragon of treachery is already in the necklace. It's already out of the box. When it's time for the golden dragon to be released, it must come out of its box first. Then it will shatter and the spirit of the dragon will enter Dexter and Jonathan. At that time the necklace will become whole again. After the dragon's power is used the spirit returns to the necklace." Reagan thought all this over and then asked,

"Dmitri and his host don't have to wait for the black dragon to come out of any box, because it's already in the necklace?"

"Yes," Daniel answered. They know where their dragon is; it's as close as the necklace around his neck. And when it's time, the spirit will enter both of them."

"Are you sure Jonathan's going to be okay?" she asked.

"He's going to be fine," he reassured her. "Now get some dry boxers on him and keep an eye on him for a while." Reagan blushed, but nodded. Daniel left the room, closing the door behind him. He stood there for a minute, thinking once again how proud he was of his son for the great job he had done that day.

Chapter Fourteen

Three weeks passed with no change in Jonathan's condition. Reagan came down the stairs and joined Daniel on the patio.

"How is he?" Daniel asked of Jonathan. Reagan shook her head.

"Still no change." She was rubbing her stomach and Daniel noticed how pale she was.

"Are you okay?" he asked.

"No, I've been feeling sick the past couple of days," she answered. She walked into the living room and sat on the couch. Daniel shook his head and let it drop.

"I should have picked up on this when you couldn't cook anything without running out of the kitchen sick. You're pregnant, aren't you?"

"I don't know," she said.

"I told you not to let your relationship go that far until after this mission was over, didn't I?" She could hear the anger in his voice. "Tomorrow I want you to go find a doctor and get tested." As they were talking they suddenly heard footsteps coming down the stairs. Both of them turned in time to see Jonathan coming into the room. Reagan quickly got up and ran to Jonathan, giving him a big hug.

Jonathan barely knew she was there.

"What's there to eat? I'm starved," he stated. Disappointed and feeling nauseous, Reagan took her arms from around his neck and ran out of the room. Jonathan watched as she ran to the bathroom. "What's wrong with her?" he asked. Daniel came across to Jonathan and gave him a hug.

"Great to have you back," he said, grinning.

"How long have I been asleep?" was Jonathan's next question.

"About three weeks," answered Daniel. Jonathan looked back towards the bathroom.

"Now what's the matter with her again?" Daniel slowly replied.

"She has a stomach flu." They walked into the kitchen to feed Jonathan's appetite. As Daniel searched the refrigerator for his son something to eat, Jonathan asked about working out. Daniel nodded.

"Sure. We can work out today if you feel up to it."

"Okay," Jonathan said. "I feel up to it, but right now I'm hungry. I haven't eaten in three weeks." He grinned and Daniel and chuckled. As he was eating he got serious again. "Daniel, something happened while I was asleep."

"Oh? What was that?" When he turned around Jonathan grabbed the plate from his hands and put it in the microwave to warm it up.

"I don't know exactly, but I know that something's different." Reagan finally came out of the bathroom and was still wiping her face with a damp cloth. She joined them at the table and Daniel was afraid what might happen if she looked at the food. No sooner had Jonathan taken his plate out and put it on the table that Reagan was running back to the bathroom. Smelling the food had the opposite effect on Jonathan as it did on Reagan. He was so hungry that he didn't even notice how she left the room. In fact, he started eating before he had reached the table with it. Daniel wasn't sure if Jonathan was eager to continue training, or where exactly his mind was, when he asked a second time:

"Will we train when I finish eating?"

"As long as you feel up to it, yes, we can train," Daniel said. They got quiet again as Jonathan continued eating. After a few minutes, Daniel broke the silence. "Do you remember anything from inside the cave?" he asked. Jonathan thought for a second.

"I remember that when I stepped into the outer circle, the air was so hot and thick that it threw me to the ground and I had trouble breathing. That's all I remember."

"If you still feel like training, we will," Daniel said. "With you being out for so long, we've lost valuable time." Jonathan quickly stuffed the last few bites in his mouth. Almost as if he was afraid Daniel would change his mind. Still chewing, he ran up the stairs to his room to change clothes.

Daniel was cleaning up the dishes when Reagan came back into the room. "You need to pull yourself together before Jonathan figures out that something's wrong," he scolded her.

"Sorry", she said. "That food just smelled disgusting."

"When do you plan on finding a doctor? The sooner the better," he suggested. She avoided eye contact with him.

"I'd like to watch Jonathan train for a little while. I want to see that he's okay. I'll go when you two are in the classroom."

Jonathan came running downstairs and right past them onto the patio. They followed him and Daniel called for Maximus. As the cheetah took his place beside Jonathan he was running in place.

"I'm going to beat you today," he told Maximus. They stood ready, waiting for Daniel to give the go ahead. Hesitating, keeping them on their toes, Daniel finally yelled, "GO!" Maximus sped off with Jonathan close behind him. By the time the cheetah made the first turn Jonathan had passed him and was nothing more than a blur. The young man ran so fast the leaves on the trees were blowing in the breeze he created. He was the first to return to the patio and knelt down with arms open wide, waiting for Maximus to return. Reagan and Daniel stood in amazement at what they were witnessing. Nearing the house and seeing Jonathan posed on the patio, Maximus slowed down. Jonathan gave him a hug and headed into the house. "That was terrific, son," Daniel said. "I expected you to be out of sorts after the cave and being asleep for so long." Reagan was standing behind him clapping.

"I told you, sir. Something has changed. Can we go to the combat chamber now?" Jonathan asked. He hurried through the door and left them all behind. Daniel and Reagan looked at each other, not really knowing what to think.

"Well," Daniel said. "I can't wait to see what he has up his sleeve in the chamber."

"What do you mean by that?" she asked him.

"It's hard to explain, but I know that what you're seeing is all Jonathan. I don't think any of this is coming from Dexter." When they arrived at the chamber Jonathan was anxiously waiting.

"Ready whenever you are," he told Daniel. "And will you please set it to the highest level?" He took a stance and spread his arms out swinging them back and forth and side to side. Daniel gave him a look.

"You're asking me to put it all the way up to maximum?" he questioned. Jonathan nodded.

"Yes, please." Jonathan focused all his attention on the chamber and Daniel hit the button turning it on. Instantly Jonathan was surrounded by so many holograms that he could barely be seen by those watching. All twenty holograms began charging and attacking him at once. Everybody inside, including Jonathan, was moving at such a high rate of speed that all the spectators could see was a blur. Reagan mused that it looked like a cloud with lots of different colors. What they couldn't see inside was how well Jonathan was holding his own. For every punch they threw he blocked them, and every kick was deflected. One by one the holograms came flying out of the cloud and landed against the glass. As the last one fell, the cloud dispersed and Daniel and Reagan could see in, their eyes grew wide, and they were in awe. But instead of exploding like they always did before, the holograms regrouped and again surrounded him. Anticipating their next move, Jonathan squatted down and waited to see what was going to happen. Suddenly, as if his enemies all had pistols, shots started coming at him from each one of their hands. Jonathan jumped up high in the air and yelled, "Fiery sword," and the sword appeared in his hand. He began spinning in midair creating a vortex. He ran around the chamber through all their fire power cutting across each body with the sword. They fell one by one, sometimes two by two. Jonathan lost count of how many of them were left. Expecting a few to still be standing when all the partial bodies came to rest, he was prepared as wire seemed to come out of his hands. Landing on his feet and seeing all his adversaries destroyed, the wire disappeared. Looking around at the mess he glanced up at Daniel and gave him a wink. Daniel turned to the control panel and switched it off. As Jonathan emerged from the chamber Daniel shook his head.

"I see you're getting cocky," he accused him. Reagan walked up to them and without really acknowledging Jonathan, she spoke to Daniel.

"I will be back later. I have those errands to run." Daniel nodded and she left the two men alone.

Daniel put his arm around Jonathan and said, "We have a lot to cover in class today. Including some more personal stuff." Jonathan looked back at the door.

"Why is she going out again?" he asked. Daniel shrugged his shoulders.

"Just running some errands, that's all," he answered. "Jonathan, I'm proud of you and all that you've accomplished up to this point. Your energy and power are outstanding. Whenever Dexter wakes up, I believe that all will be revealed to you. And the time for that to happen is just about at hand." They walked into the classroom and sat down. "I mentioned to you about a couple of new techniques. There is another one called the shield. This one can only be used to cover the neuron bomb. Dexter will be able to help you with this as well." Daniel hesitated. "There's something very important I need to tell you. I'm going to need all your attention." Jonathan could tell that Daniel was tensing up and saw him wrenching his hands together. "There is no easy way for me to say this. I've thought many times the best time and way to tell you. Many years ago I was caught by what I thought was a routine traffic stop. Instead, I was grabbed from behind and no matter how hard I wanted to I couldn't fight whoever it was. Then I was thrown into the air. I knew when I landed I would probably have broken bones. Instead, I found myself here. Just as you did. The keepers of the gate selected me to train you when the time came." He paused and took a deep breath. "Since it was necessary for me to travel extensively between the realms they changed my appearance. How you see me now is not how I looked back then. They didn't want to risk me being recognized. Once I began studying the scrolls and realizing what was to come, my dedication was solely for saving the earth. It was hard leaving my family. My wife, son and daughter." Jonathan became full of curiosity.

"What are you trying to tell me? Who is it you're talking about?" he asked. Daniel took another deep breath and swallowed hard.

"Jonathan, you're my son." Jonathan's face was full of confusion and denial as he started to cry.

"Why are you telling me this?" he cried.

"I'm sorry. It's the truth and you need to know. I should have told you before now. I didn't want to be a distraction from your training."

"Why didn't you try to come see us?" he yelled at his father. He stood up and began pacing the floor. "My mother struggled to raise us. Alone."

"Jonathan, I had to do what was right for the world, just like you do right now. I had no choice. They wouldn't let me come back. I had to accept it and do what was needed." Daniel stood up and grabbed his son, forcing him to look him in the eye.

"Listen to me. You have to know that what I'm telling you is the truth. Look where we are right now. We will have to fight together to save our world. Jonathan, it's been extremely hard to stand back and keep quiet until the appropriate time. Watching my children grow up without me. And yes, I watched Katherine struggle." Jonathan cut him off before he could say anymore.

"It was hard for me too. Hard to understand that all of a sudden you were gone." He grabbed his father and hugged him tighter than even he expected of himself. Daniel held his son as he cried.

"We're here now, son. Working together to save the world."

Chapter Fifteen

Daniel sat on the patio and watched his son train. Jonathan was using the fiery swords, and Daniel was amazed. He could tell that every time Jonathan trained, he put a little more into it. Reagan walked outside and Daniel saw that she was holding maternity pamphlets.

"I'm assuming everything went well, or didn't it?" he asked.

"The doctor said I'm about three weeks along." She stood beside him and watched Jonathan.

"What are you going to do?" he asked. Reagan shook her head.

"I don't know," was her reply.

"Well, Reagan, telling him right now would startle him. You can't tell him yet." They stood there in silence. After a few minutes had passed Daniel looked at her.

"So I'm going to be a grandfather, is that right?"

"Yes," she nodded. Tears began trickling down her face. Daniel put his arm around her shoulder.

"Wait until everything is complete before telling him. We've talked about how distractions could harm him. I followed your advice and just a little while ago I told him that I was his father. You and Maximus were right. Jonathan has a right to know and he needs to know that he has family to support him. You're a part of this as well. You've been instrumental in his training and he'll need your support too."

"I can't wait to tell him," she said. "He's going to flip when he hears the news." They got silent and watched Jonathan wielding the swords. He lost one when he threw it up into the air, but never missing a beat, he continued using the remaining sword.

"Look at him. He's been at this for almost three hours." Suddenly Jonathan lost the second sword and went down on one knee and was breathing hard. "Take a break!" Daniel shouted to him.

"No," Jonathan shouted back. He caught his breath and stood up. When he did he held out his hands and both swords came up from the ground right back into his hands. He went on training with them as if he'd never lost a beat. In his head Jonathan started talking to Dexter. "If you can hear me Dexter, your brother is out there somewhere and we have to stop him. I will do all I can to bring you back, but once that happens we have got to take him out."

"Take a break, Jonathan," Daniel shouted. Turning to Reagan he said, "If he knew you were here he'd stop and take a break." She blushed.

"What is that supposed to mean?" she asked. When he grinned at her, she yelled to Jonathan. "Come get a drink of water, at least." Hearing Reagan's voice, Jonathan put down his hands and the swords disappeared. He ran to the patio to join the others. Daniel and Reagan shared another glance at seeing that Daniel was right. Daniel laughed and went inside.

"Hey," Jonathan said, coming up to stand beside Reagan. She handed him a glass of water.

"You've been working hard this afternoon, so I've been told."

"Yeah, but it's different now," he said. Reagan wiped some sweat from his brow.

"Come inside and get a towel." She started to lead the way inside, but quickly realized he wasn't following her. She turned around to see him heading back out to train. Before he could get too far she grabbed his hand and pulled him into the house. She got him a towel and he dried his face. She leaned in and gave him a long kiss. Jonathan didn't pull away, but his mind was still on training.

"I want to go the weight room for a bit," he said.

"No," Reagan insisted. "You can't spend every minute training. And besides, I'd like to spend some time together." He always found her hard to resist so he quit trying. She grabbed him by the hand and they walked to the living room. She sat on the couch, but Jonathan wouldn't sit beside her because he was still hot and sweaty. He sat on the floor leaning against the couch between her knees. Thinking of what Daniel had said earlier, she asked him, "What happened while I was gone?" Jonathan bent his head back so that it was on the couch and looked up at Reagan.

"My dad is in his room," he confided. When she didn't show any emotion to his declaration, he sat up straight, turned around and got face to face with her. "Did you know about this?" he asked. Reagan's eyes dropped. "Look at me," he said, and asked again. "Did you know about this?" She still didn't answer. Jonathan stood up. "Since you won't answer that, then tell me how long you've known," he demanded. She finally replied.

"I haven't known for very long. Daniel told me after you'd been here a few weeks." She stood up and put her hand on his face. Jonathan remained silent. "I promise, Jonathan, I haven't known all that long."

"I trusted that as much as we've been through and mean to each other that you would never hide anything from me," he said. "I can handle the news that he's my father, and I understand why he waited to tell me." He removed her hand from his cheek and held it over his heart. "Please don't ever keep anything from me," he pleaded. Reagan thought back on her conversation with Daniel about her pregnancy and not telling Jonathan.

"I will never keep anything from you," she promised. He smiled at her.

"I love you so much," he said, almost in a whisper. She hugged him tight.

"I love you too," she said in a soft voice. He stepped back and held both her hands in his.

"So where did you go today?" he asked her. She hesitated before answering.

"I went to get stuff for the house. Ice cream and snacks and stuff," she said. She breathed a sigh of relief at being able to come up with a quick answer.

"Ice cream!" Jonathan shrieked as he ran to the kitchen. Reagan was right behind him as he opened the freezer door. As fast as she could she closed the door.

"This is my ice cream," she said, blocking the door.

"I thought you said these snacks were for the house," he reminder her. He tried again to get the ice cream, but nearly got his arm caught in the freezer door. "Well, what other snacks did you get?" he asked.

"Look in the refrigerator," she told him. Knowing there weren't really any snacks to be found in there, she feared he would catch on to her. "Oh, all right," she exclaimed. She shut the door to the refrigerator before he could look in it. He looked up at her like she'd lost her mind. She opened the freezer, grabbed the ice cream and gave it to him.

"Here," she said. "But don't eat it all." Jonathan got a bowl out of the cabinet and filled it. "Don't you think that's enough?" Reagan cried as she grabbed the ice cream from him. She put the top on the container and put it back in the freezer.

"No," he was saying. "I wasn't done with that." She gave him a fake look of anger and he gave her one as well.

"Yes, you are. Now get on out of the kitchen so I can fix dinner," she ordered. She pushed him out the door.

"I'm going to my room," he said. Ice cream in hand, he trotted up the steps to his room. Sitting on the bed and digging into the ice cream, he looked up and noticed the pants hanging in the closet. They were the pants he was wearing the night of the explosion. He thought back on that night and suddenly jumped up and reached for the pants. He remembered the wallet that he had picked up on the stairs that night. Reagan had washed the pants, but hadn't noticed the wallet. Jonathan looked at the contents. There was a card inside that hadn't totally survived the wash, but hadn't been totally destroyed, either. He could make out the right side of the card and the word Enterprises. Jonathan sat down on the bed thinking and, still hoping to make out more of the writing on the card, he set the wallet on the table by his bed and left the room.

He ran back downstairs to the kitchen. Reagan was ready to defend her kitchen again. He needed to stay out so she could fix dinner. Before she could scold him, he asked, "Have you seen Daniel?" She thought for a moment.

"Have you checked his room? I expect that's where he is," she suggested. Before she could say another word, Jonathan had already left the room. He went all over the mansion searching for his father. He checked Daniel's room, the classroom to no avail, before finding him in the weapons room. He was taking inventory.

"So this is where you are," Jonathan said as he entered the room. "I've been looking all over for you." Daniel turned around to face Jonathan and took off his glasses.

"What is it?" he asked. Handing Daniel the card, he said,

"Take a look at this and see what you make of it." Daniel looked the card over and then up at Jonathan.

"You're going to have to give me some time so I can put this together on the computer." Jonathan nodded.

"How long will that take?" he asked. Daniel shrugged his shoulders.

"Hard to tell, really. Could be a few days, could take a couple of weeks," was his reply. "We'll give it a try and see what we come up with."

"Thanks," Jonathan said as he turned and headed for the door. Daniel stopped him.

"We'll breeze through the weapons and vehicle training. We need to get you and Reagan back to school. I've already explained to her that when you go back, only three days will have passed. Ya'll are really going to have to keep your eyes open. This could get really ugly before it's all over. Oh, and the funerals for your mother and Caroline will be on Friday."

Jonathan nodded. He knew now that his family being murdered hurt Daniel as much as it did him.

"What makes you say that it could get ugly?" he asked. Daniel picked up the card and looked at it again.

"Whoever or whatever is behind this, I have a feeling this card is going to clue us in on a big part of it. We have about another month to train and then we'll begin looking for Dmitri."

Chapter Sixteen

Reagan and Jonathan came out of the mansion headed back to school. What was actually three months to them was only three days back home. Daniel joined them out front, holding Jonathan's golden necklace.

"You two be careful and keep your eyes open," Daniel commanded. Jonathan gave him a cocky grin.

"Don't worry Dad," he said. "I'll be okay and I'll make sure Reagan is too." Daniel loved hearing Jonathan call him dad. He hugged his son tight, as he used to do many years ago. Jonathan hugged him back and faced the car. "Doors open," he commanded and the doors of the golden lion opened and the two students got in.

"So what do you think will happen when they see me back in school?" Reagan asked. Jonathan gave her a worried chuckle.

"Don't worry about that. It won't be you they'll be looking at. It was my house that blew up. And remember,

Krista thinks I was inside when it happened." He gave another
command, "Start," and the ignition started. Jonathan backed
out of the driveway and drove off.

"Remember what Daniel said about the portal." Reagan
pointed to one of them any buttons on the car's dash. "When
you pass the oak tree press this one," she said. He was
beginning to get annoyed with her. He gave her a stern look.

"I know. I was in the training, remember?" he snapped.
The portal opened and driving through it put them out onto a
back road behind where Jonathan had lived. He began looking
around nervously.

"Relax," Reagan told him. She reached her hand up to
the back of his neck and started rubbing it. It wasn't long
before the school was in sight. "Look, there's the school," she
pointed out. Stopped at the stop sign, Jonathan took a deep
breath. When he continued to sit there, Reagan looked at him.
His grip on the steering wheel was so tight she could see the
veins in his hands.

"I really don't want to go back to this school," he told
her. Reagan took her hand from his neck and gently touched
his cheek.

"Don't be afraid," she said. "You know this is part of
the mission. You're more than just a senior in high school now.

The fate of the world depends on you. I know you'll be fine."
He took her hand from his cheek and gently kissed her palm.

"I love you," he said. Reluctantly he drove to the
school. Jonathan looked around as they passed the football
field. "Can you believe it's only been three days since we were
here?" He pulled into a parking space and shut the car off.

"Doors open," Reagan said. The car doors opened but
she was the only one that got out. She looked at the driver's
side and Jonathan was just sitting there gazing at the school. It
felt old, but it also felt new. She walked around to his side of
the car and pulled him out. "Get out, now," she ordered.

They walked across the parking lot hand in hand and
headed to the cafeteria. Reagan tried to lead him up the stairs to
the main hall. Jonathan hesitated.

"I think we should go to the principal's office first to let
them know I'm back. We don't know if they think I died with
my family that night." As they walked along they passed some
blue benches that stretched the length of the main building. As
they got closer to them, they came up on Charles, but he had his
back to them. The young lady he was talking to stopped and
stared at Jonathan as if she was seeing a ghost. Turning to see
what she was looking at, Charles found himself face to face
with his best friend. He threw his arms around Jonathan.

"Man, people all over town thought you died in that explosion," Charles said, excitedly.

"No," Jonathan replied. "Here I am in the flesh." Charles was hugging his friend so tight, that Jonathan had to wiggle to get loose so he could breathe. "What's been going on these last few months?" he asked. Reagan poked him in the side to remind him the times were different.

"What do you mean few months?" Charles asked, confused. Jonathan shook his head.

"Sorry," he said. "I meant the last few days. My mind is still sort of muddled." Charles nodded. He knew this wasn't an easy time for his best friend. Especially with the funerals coming up.

"It's been a mess around here," he explained. "The whole school has been in an uproar about you and your family. We'll be there tomorrow. We're here for you, you know that." Jonathan shook Charles' hand.

"Thanks," he said.

"Just wait until everybody sees you, Buddy. They are going to be shocked." He was looking at Jonathan, checking him out. "You've put on some weight. And that brings me to another question. Where the heck have you been? How come we're just now hearing from you?" Jonathan shot a quick glance at Reagan. Before she could help come up with an answer, he told his friend, "I've been staying with Reagan and her family." Charles studied Reagan for a minute or so.

"Wait a minute," he started. "Aren't you the girl that walked past us in the parking lot the first day of school?" Reagan nodded and smiled. "Where are you headed?" he asked, looking back at Jonathan.

"Headed to the principal's office to make sure I'm still a student here. With everybody thinking…, you know…I don't want to just walk into class. Where are you headed?"

Going to go ride around town for a bit, then I'll be back. Let's meet after first period, okay?" Jonathan chuckled and shook his head.

"I see some things haven't changed." The kids went their separate ways. Jonathan opened the door and Reagan led the way down the hallway to the main office. She stopped at the door to the office and let Jonathan go in first. He walked up to the desk. "Hello, Mrs. Jones," he said. The secretary was startled when she looked up at him.

"You're alive!" she exclaimed.

"Yes, ma'am. Is Principle Eden in?" he asked. "I wanted to make sure everything was all right before I just showed up in class."

"No, he's not," she answered. "Let me check in the computer. Everything's fine, Mr. Valedictorian. You're still a student here." Jonathan smiled and relaxed a little.

"So I can go to my classes?" he asked.

"Yes, you can," she said with a smile. Jonathan thanked her and they turned to leave. As he turned around he could see through the glass doors that Krista and Michael were headed their way. If he and Reagan left the office right then they would bump into them, so he grabbed Reagan's arm and made her wait. Jonathan timed it so that they would end up walking behind Michael and Krista. Thinking they were out of earshot as they exited the main hallway, Reagan spoke to Jonathan.

"I hope they don't turn around," she said. No such luck. Krista heard a voice and turned to see who was behind her. Upon seeing Jonathan, she forgot about being with Michael, her eyes grew wide and she threw her arms around him.

"Jonathan," she screamed. He didn't hesitate to pull her arms from around his neck. He looked beside him to see Reagan standing with arms crossed looking angry. She was glaring at Krista. Out of the corner of his eye he saw a punch coming at him from his childhood nemesis. Before it connected, Jonathan caught Michael's fist and started to squeeze it. The bully was caught off guard as he had never seen Jonathan defend himself before. Not only was he defending himself, he had such strength now that he could easily have broken Michael's hand. Reagan slapped Jonathan in the back.

"Let him go," she ordered. Jonathan looked at her for a second before turning back to Michael and slapping him in the chest. It was a hard enough slap that it sent him stumbling backward.

"That will be enough," Jonathan told him. "I don't want to hurt you." Michael stood there holding his chest and tried to catch his breath. The embarrassment showed in his face as he saw the big crowd that had gathered to see Jonathan rough him up. Jonathan grabbed Reagan by the shoulders and they walked past the other two and headed to class.

"I bet he won't try that again," remarked Reagan. Jonathan sighed.

"I really didn't want to do that," he admitted. "Listen, Reagan. Keep a really close eye on Krista when the two of you go to PE class. Things just don't feel right around here," he said. "Everyone's acting weird."

"I would be too if I thought you had been blown up in an explosion and you suddenly came back to life," she retorted.

"Find out anything you can and I'll meet you in front of Mr. Eden's office before we go to English Composition. I'll keep an eye on Charles and Michael," he said.

"Why those two?" Reagan questioned. Jonathan explained.

"Michael is with Krista and I'm not sure why. And you saw how Charles acted when he first saw me, didn't you? He was nervous and fidgety. When it comes right down to it, anybody could be involved. There's not really anybody that we can count out." They sat down on a bench outside the science department.

"What would you do if you find that Charles is involved?" she asked him. Jonathan gave the question some thought before answering her.

"I truly hope that he's not involved, but if he is, he will die. There are so many possibilities and we don't really know much yet."

"That's why we have to take our time and go about all of this carefully and meticulously," she agreed. Looking out over the parking lot, something caught Jonathan's eye. He patted Reagan's arm.

"Look at that," he said, pointing. They both watched as Charles frantically shoved a big black bag into his car and drove off.

"What do you suppose that was all about?" Reagan asked. Jonathan shrugged his shoulders.

"I don't know, but it sure makes me want to keep a closer eye on him. We know Krista's involved, so we'll definitely keep an eye on her," he said. He noticed she was rubbing her stomach. "What's the matter?" he asked.

"Nothing," she quickly replied. "I'm just hungry."

"Didn't you eat breakfast before we left the house?" Jonathan wanted to know.

"Yes, I did. But I'm hungry again, okay?" He noticed she was getting a little attitude.

"You sure have been getting defensive a lot lately," he said. "And I don't understand why half the time." Reagan didn't respond. "We'll talk about this later," he said. They stood up and went to class.

Chapter Seventeen

Gym class was over and Reagan was getting books from her locker. As she closed it she heard Krista's voice, but she didn't recognize the voice of the male she was talking to. Looking around, Reagan spied the laundry basket. She quickly ducked behind it so as not to be seen.

"You're telling me Jonathan's alive?" asked the male voice. Krista nodded her head.

"Yes, Jason, he is. Michael and I bumped into him first thing this morning," she replied, nervously.

"Dmitri had a feeling Jonathan didn't perish in that explosion." He took his cell phone out of his pants pocket and dialed Dmitri's number. "Sir, you were right. It's just as you said. Jonathan is still alive. How do you want us to proceed?" After a brief pause, he looked at Krista and spoke again. "Yes, sir. I understand. We'll get right on it." He put the phone back in his pocket and ran his hands through his hair.

"What did he say?" Krista wanted to know.

"Just to lay low and keep out of sight for the time being," Jason answered. Krista looked around the room as if she were looking for someone.

"Jonathan was with some girl today," she told Jason. "She's new here. I've never seen her before. She was here the day of the explosion. There's something suspicious about her." The concern showed in Jason's face.

"Do you know her name?" he questioned. Krista shook her head.

"No, I don't. You know, Jonathan looked different today. He looked more muscular and his hair has grown quite a bit too."

"Is there anybody else at this school that could be a problem for us?" Jason asked. After giving it some thought Krista replied.

"His friend Charles could be a problem for us."

"Do you know where he lives?" asked Jason. She nodded.

"He lives over on Adams Street. Actually, it's right around the corner from my house. It's the biggest house on the block and the only one that's brick. You can't miss it." Jason pulled his phone out of his pocket and dialed a number.

"Go to Adams Street and look for the only brick house on the street. Keep everyone in the house alive, but bring Charles with you," he instructed the person on the other end of the phone. He gave Krista a confused look. "Should he be here at school?"

"Yes," she said. "But because of his dad Charles often leaves during the day. His family is very wealthy." Speaking to the phone once again Jason gave further instructions.

"If no one is there when you get to the house, wait until they return. And take some backup with you in case there's trouble." Jason put his phone away and stood silent, as if he were concentrating. Reagan had a sudden feeling that he could sense her presence. She did everything but hold her breath to make sure she wasn't detected. Jason turned back to Krista. "Let's go so we can get this plan into motion." The two of them walked out of the room. Reagan waited a minute or two before coming out from behind the basket. She grabbed her bag and slowly made her way to the exit door. She wanted to give them plenty of time to leave before she left herself. When she got to the door, she slowly pushed it open, looking both directions to make sure the coast was clear. Upon seeing no one, she walked out the door. No sooner had she stepped foot out into the hallway than Jason grabbed her from behind. He held her while Krista put a piece of tape over Reagan's mouth. Their captive kicked violently trying hard to break free, but Jason's grip was too much for her. As they quickly exited the building a black car sped up to the curb. Reagan continued to fight as hard as she could, to no avail. Krista opened the back door so Jason could put Reagan in the car. Just before Jason got in the car himself, he looked around to make sure nobody had seen what had just happened. With no windows in the gym, he was certain there were no witnesses. As the car sped off, Michael emerged from behind a tree across the street. He had seen Krista with this strange man and was spying on her in an attempt to find out who the man was and what they were up to. In a panic, Michael started running. The only thing he could think to do was to tell the principle what he had just seen. In his frenzy and not paying attention to anything around him he ran smack into Jonathan. Jonathan gave him a look of irritation and asked him,

"What do you want Michael?" Still in a panic, Michael was breathing heavy, and tried hard to catch his breath. He had to repeat himself before Jonathan could understand a word he was saying. "Slow down, Michael so I can hear you. What are you talking about?"

"Your girlfriend was just kidnapped! Krista and some man I didn't know put her into a black car and sped off! He could see the fire rise up in Jonathan's face.

"Which way did they go?" he asked. Jonathan was about on the verge of panic himself. "You said it was a black car. What else can you tell me?" Still breathing a bit heavy, Michael told Jonathan what little he knew.

"It was a four door sedan with dark windows. I want to say it was a Cadillac. I didn't get a good look at the guy, all I saw was his hair was dark. Could have been black. After they pulled out of the parking lot, I don't know which way they went." Jonathan reached for his phone and called Daniel. He finally answered after the third ring. Jonathan explained everything he had been told.

"I'm headed back to the mansion, but first I'm going to ask Michael some questions," he told Daniel. He hung up and turned to Michael, who was just now starting to breathe normally. However, he was still in a state of confusion because of all this. "Michael, in the time that you've been with Krista has she acted weird at any time?" Michael nodded his head.

"Yeah, lately she's been really distant and wanting her own space," he explained. The two young men walked around the outside of the cafeteria headed for the parking lot.

"What do you mean her own space?" Jonathan asked.

"She didn't want to do anything anymore. I know this doesn't make sense, but it's almost like she had been hypnotized or something." Michael hung his head. He still wasn't sure what to make of all that had happened the last few days. "Jonathan, she's been very violent lately too. Things she never liked to do before, now she wants to do them", he said.

"What do you mean by that?" Jonathan asked.

"She never liked horror films and hunting, but for a while now, that's all she ever wants to do," Michael told him. You could almost see the light bulb above Jonathan's head.

"You mentioned that she seemed hypnotized. That's it!" he exclaimed. "He has her in a trance or something." Michael gave him an odd look.

"What are you talking about?" he demanded to know. Without answering, Jonathan trotted to his car.

"Open trunk," he commanded. When the trunk opened he reached in and grabbed a homing device. He ran back to Michael. "Give me your watch." Even more confused, Michael did as he was instructed. As quickly as he could Jonathan opened the back to the time piece and inserted the device. As he handed Michael back his watch, he told him, "Wear this all the time, and don't ever take it off."

"What was it that you put inside my watch?" Michael asked.

"It's a homing device that will help protect you. No matter where you are I'll be able to keep up with you. If anybody saw you and knows you witnessed what happened, they may come looking for you. Whatever you do, don't take off your watch!" Michael nodded, scratched his head and looked at Jonathan.

"Who are you?" he asked with great curiosity. "Or better yet, WHAT are you?"

"Don't worry about that, Michael. If they got a look at you, you're going to need this. Those people are very dangerous. I'm going to need your cooperation."

"Okay," Michael nodded. "What do you need from me?" he asked reluctantly.

"If something happens to you, you need to turn your watch back one hour. That activates the homing device."

"So that's all I have to do?" Michael asked. "Just turn it back, right?" Jonathan nodded.

"Yes, that's right. Now it's acting as the battery, but when you turn it back, the homing device kicks in."

"Jonathan, what do you think they're going to do with her?" Michael asked.   Jonathan hung his head.

"I don't know," he said. "But when I find them, I assure you, they will all die."   He ran to the Golden Lion and got in. On his way out of the parking lot he stopped beside Michael.

"Be careful, Michael. Those same people may come back. And don't tell anyone about anything that happened today."

"Why not?" he asked. Jonathan shook his head and gave Michael a serious look.

"We don't need the school in an uproar over something they won't understand and that I can take care of. Trust me, I can handle this." They waved at each other and Jonathan drove off. He spoke out loud. "Dial the mansion." When Daniel answered the phone Jonathan told him he was on his way. "Daniel I need you to call Charles. If he's at home, tell him to stay there."

"Okay," was his reply. "Did you get any lead on Reagan's whereabouts?"

"No," said Jonathan. "But I put a homing device inside Michael's watch and that might help us."

"Do you think they'll come after him?" Daniel asked.

"I don't know, but if they do it should lead us right to Dmitri." Jonathan hit the dashboard with his fist. "We have GOT to find her!"

"Jonathan, there's no answer at Charles' house," Daniel said. Jonathan's grip on the steering wheel tightened. He hung up the phone and spoke to the car.

"Golden Eagle," was the command he gave. The car continued to move as the wheels turned in and wings emerged from the sides. Before he could be seen he gave the command "Golden stealth." As the boosters engaged and he became airborne Jonathan gave a loud, "Woo hoo," and sped off to find Charles. Jonathan could think of nothing except for watching Charles put that bag in his car that morning. He hoped more than anything that his best friend wasn't involved in any of this.

Chapter Eighteen

Jonathan arrived at Charles' house and hovered above it to be safe. When he didn't see any movement, he came out of stealth mode and landed the Golden Lion.   Every move he made was cautious. Slowly he made his way to the front door, constantly looking in every direction for anything out of the ordinary. When his knocks went unanswered he went to the window to look in. Seeing that the living room had been ransacked, he kicked in the door. He shouted Charles' name several times, getting no response. The place was in ruins. There wasn't a piece of furniture that was left untouched. Everything was knocked over, contents from all the drawers and cabinets were strewn all over, and every lamp was broken. It was a large house and Jonathan went through every room, finding them all in the same condition.   He searched every inch in hopes of finding someone, anyone, alive and hiding. Going through the bedrooms he found the beds turned over and mattresses cut open. Jonathan had never seen such devastation.

He headed back downstairs towards the dining room. Pretty sure of what he would find, he suddenly had an eerie feeling. As he reached the door to the dining room, he ducked. Jonathan's instincts were correct, as a man took a hard swing at him. As he ducked he quickly rolled across the floor and got to his feet. Backing up to put more room between them and protect his back, Jonathan found himself looking at three men rather than just the one. He was the first to speak.

"I'm only going to ask this once. Where is my friend?" He kept a close eye on them.

"Either dead or with Dmitri," replied one of the men. Jonathan was clenching his fists. "Either way you're going to join him", the man continued. Before any of them could speak another word, Jonathan sprang into action. He jumped at them punching the first one in the face, sending him backwards into the wall. The second one received an unmerciful kick to the crotch, sending him to the floor. Jonathan grabbed the last man, held him up against the wall and asked again about Charles' whereabouts. The man on the floor was slowly attempting to get to his feet. In the blink of an eye, Jonathan threw a paralyzing dart hitting him directly in the chest. He fell to his knees shaking, but still alive with eyes wide open. Jonathan focused once again on the man he had against the wall.

"I'm going to ask you again. You give me the right answer or you're finished." He pulled a small silver device from his pocket. "Any idea what this is?" he asked.   Getting no answer Jonathan put the device against the man's arm. "Let me explain what it is," Jonathan said calmly as the man screamed in pain. This is a bomb that will blow you and this house up at the push of a button. Now, where is he?" In between cries and painful breaths, the man answered.

"He's been taken to Dmitri," he admitted.

"Where is his hideout and what is he planning?" Jonathan demanded to know.   "Tell me the truth and I just may allow you to live." As he was interrogating the man, Jonathan noticed out the back window that four more men were walking through the backyard towards the house.

The first man he punched had called for help. Jonathan took the one he was interrogating and threw him through the window, hitting one of the four men, knocking him to the ground. He then ran to the backyard to meet the newcomers. As he ran out the door he saw a table saw coming straight at him. One of them threw it, but Jonathan was able to dodge it in time. As it passed by his face, he caught it and hurled it back at the one that threw it at him, cutting the man in half.

Jonathan yelled, "Fiery swords," and the swords appeared in his hands. The three remaining men charged Jonathan and one of them met his demise as a sword pierced his abdomen. With two men left Jonathan had to come up with a plan as they suddenly had swords of their own. He needed to keep one of them alive in order to find Dmitri's hideout. One of the men came at Jonathan, and they engaged in a sword fight. The second man swung his sword at Jonathan's head. Seeing it coming he ducked and Dmitri's men came sword to sword in a fiery clash, creating sparks.

Jonathan became aware of the possibility of neighbors seeing the battle. As the two men realized they were swinging at each other, Jonathan got rid of his swords and began running circles around them. His speed steadily increased until he ran so fast that they were unable to see him. They started to panic as the blur created the illusion of a wall that they couldn't break through.

As he ran, Jonathan released a rope made of a titanium alloy. He wrapped the two men back to back so tightly that they couldn't keep their balance and fell over. They tried to break free with no luck. They looked up to see their captor walk towards them and kneel down on one knee. He pointed to the man who he had thrown through the window earlier. "Do you two see your friend over there? Do you see the silver bug in his arm?" He asked them. He explained, "That bug is strong enough to take out this house and all of you with it. You've already wasted my time, so I'm going to ask you this one time and one time only. Where was my friend taken?" The men remained silent.

True to his word, Jonathan only asked once. He got up and walked into the house. He kept thinking there had to be a clue inside somewhere. He walked back upstairs realizing he hadn't gone through every room. He went to Charles' bedroom and was surprised that it was in pristine condition. This didn't make sense. Why would they ransack the house but leave one room untouched? Being very cautious and alert in case of another ambush, Jonathan began searching the entire room looking for any clue that could give him answers about Charles.

He looked in every corner, under every piece of furniture and even checked the closet very carefully. He decided to check out the drawers in the dresser and in the top one found a set of blueprints. Jonathan wasn't an expert at reading blueprints, but he was certain they looked like some sort of fortress. He took his phone out of his pocket and dialed Daniel's number.

"Hello?" answered Daniel.

"Hey Dad, it's me," Jonathan began. "When we were younger, wasn't Charles' father an architect?"

"Yes, he was," Daniel replied. "Why do you ask? Did you find something?"

"Yeah, I found some blueprints and they really look like they are for a hideout of some sort."

"What about Charles? Did you find him?" Daniel asked.

"No," was Jonathan's reply. "They took him. I'm wondering if they were expecting someone else because there were a couple of them still here when I got here. If Mr. Bradley plays some part in all of this, that could be why they took Charles. I'm on my way back there. We'll try and figure this out. Were you able to find anything on that card I gave you?"

"Not as of yet," Daniel answered. "The computer is still working on decoding it."

"I'll see you in a few minutes," Jonathan said before hanging up. He tucked the blueprints under his arm and cautiously walked downstairs and out the front door. With every step he took, he could feel the anger building up inside him. He sat in the car and hung his head. Not knowing where Charles and Reagan had been taken was driving him crazy. He started the car, put it in stealth mode and hovered a few houses away. Tears ran down his cheek as he spoke out loud. "Sorry Charles," he said, in almost a whisper. He pushed the button on the console and the house exploded. He watched it and noticed the neighbors coming out of their houses in a panic. Jonathan shook his head and drove off. His thoughts remained on finding his best friend and the love of his life and what he would do to Dmitri when he found him. Just thinking about Reagan being abducted made Jonathan's heart feel numb. As he drove through the portal he said to himself, "Hold on,

Reagan. I'll find you."

Chapter Nineteen

Jonathan parked the Golden Lion in the garage and quickly got out. He was anxious to find Daniel and start sorting out what all had happened today. He searched every room where he thought his Dad would be and finally found him in the classroom. Daniel was sitting in front of his laptop.

"Have a seat, son. I have some things I need to tell you," Daniel said. "You may not want to hear this, and it may come as a shock to you. But I need to tell you everything." Jonathan noticed the frown on Daniel's face. "First off, the situation with Charles…you remembered correctly. His father was an architect. That's how he made his fortune. He designed some of the biggest and most impressive buildings in the country. As you know, he's still a very wealthy man. Unfortunately when I was a detective, I busted Mr. Bradley for money laundering. Being that he was a friend of mine and our sons were best friends, I covered it up for him as long as he promised to shut down his business. He agreed and his wife never knew about it. There were still people, however, that were upset with him." Daniel breathed a sigh.

"Where does Dmitri come into this?" Jonathan asked.

"The best I can figure is that Dmitri had Gary design something for him. I'm assuming Charles was taken as an insurance policy to use against his father," Daniel continued. "With so much happening right now, it looks like Dmitri is gathering up everybody he feels he needs to because he's figured out that Dexter is inside you. It could be that he's abducting people close to you because it's you he needs insurance against. It would also serve as a distraction that could make you mess up to Dmitri's advantage."

"He has Reagan," Jonathan said emphatically as he hung his head.

"I know, son," Daniel nodded. "That's hard for me too."

"Reagan AND Charles." Jonathan sighed.

"We have got to keep our eyes and ears open. Whoever Dmitri is using, he could be standing beside us at any given time," Daniel reminded him. "The safety of the two of them is what we have to keep in mind. I don't think Dmitri wants to kill them just yet. We also need to focus on who it could be that he's indwelled himself in," Daniel went on to say. "We know what type of person we should be looking for."

"Why do you say that?" Jonathan asked him.

"Think about it," Daniel started to explain. "Dexter picked you because of your pure heart. You care about people and doing what's right. Dmitri would want someone the opposite of that. Someone who already has evil in his heart and some motivation."

"Are you saying that whoever it is, that he has a part in this too?" Jonathan queried.

"Exactly what I'm saying. Remember, Jonathan, you were chosen. You weren't tempted by or promised power or wealth. To be used this way by Dmitri, this mystery person would have to have been in agreement." Jonathan was pacing the floor.

"Do you think that Mr. Bradley could be responsible for all of this?" he asked. Daniel nodded.

"I'd say he's our number one suspect right now", Daniel replied. "So far all clues lead to him, but don't make any sudden moves just yet. He's just a suspect right now." Jonathan explained to his father what all he found at the Bradley house and what all had happened there.

"It was weird that the place was torn apart except for Charles' room. And then finding the blueprints," Jonathan explained. Daniel walked over and they both studied the diagrams.

"Whatever it is," Daniel said, "It's massive. Whoever Dmitri is using has to be rich. Not just anybody could afford to build something of this magnitude. This looks to be about four times bigger than the mansion." They continued to study the blueprints in amazement. "Son, I don't mean to change the subject, but are you planning on going to the memorial service for your Mother and sister?" He could see the hurt and anger rise up in Jonathan's face. He was thinking about Daniel's question but never answered him. Daniel continued, "Jonathan, you really should go. It would provide some closure for you. A chance to say goodbye."

"There won't be any closure for me until whoever did this is caught and dead", Jonathan finally replied.

"You need to reconsider," Daniel said. "Whoever it is, I'd be willing to bet that they'll be at the service." Jonathan walked over to the desk and sat down. He put his head down resting in his hands.

"Dad, how much can one man take?" he asked. Daniel grabbed a chair and pulled up beside his son. "I'm only eighteen, still a kid in some respect, and all these horrific things keep happening."

"Jonathan, even when you thought your life was ordinary things weren't perfect. Good and bad things happen in life and they all serve to make us stronger. Yes, it will be worse for someone in your present position with your power." Daniel knew what Jonathan was feeling and tried to come up with the right words to comfort and explain things. "I know it's hard to understand right now, but fate has a way of explaining things in the future. When this battle is over, we will have more time to explore your being. Who Dexter is and how this all came to include our family. Everything will fall into place for you," Daniel said.

"I miss Mom and Caroline," Jonathan said, as tears started trickling down his cheeks. Daniel patted his son on the back.

"I know," he replied, reassuringly. "And you've had to put your feelings on hold for the good of the mission and the world. And it's not over yet." Jonathan lowered his head almost to the table right beside the laptop. Just as he did, the laptop began ringing. "What on earth is that?" asked Daniel. He jumped up to get a better look at the computer.

"I think it's the homing device I put in Michael's watch in case he was also taken," Jonathan explained. I hoped if that

happened it would show us where their hideout was located."
Realizing the possibility of knowing their location, Daniel
practically yanked Jonathan out of his chair so he could get to
the computer. He checked the coordinates as quickly as he
could type them in.

"Look at this, son," he said, looking up as Jonathan was
pointing at the screen.

"Dad, do you see what I see? Am I seeing this right?"
he asked.

"Yes, I do. And yes, you are correct. That signal is
coming directly from where our house used to be. Grab the
blueprints real quick." Jonathan ran so quickly that he almost
knocked over the whole table. He spread them out for Daniel to
look at. After perusing them again, he brought the visual up on
the screen again. "Check this out," he said. "These blueprints
match the picture on the computer perfectly."

"I see that and I'm headed there now," Jonathan
exclaimed. He hurriedly ran for the door. Daniel tried to grab
him, but wasn't fast enough.

"Wait Jonathan," he yelled. "You can't go running over
there without a plan. You can't just go waltzing into some
crazed lunatic's lair. Plus you have a memorial service to
attend tomorrow morning, or has that slipped your mind?

Remember, Dmitri has the black dragon." Jonathan stood by the door looking at his father.

"I don't care," he told him. Daniel walked toward the door.

"Trust me Jonathan, please," he began. "I know how badly you want to race over there. And part of me would love for you to go, but pay your family your respects first." Jonathan knew Daniel was right. He dropped his head and walked away from the door. "Do you really think it would be wise to go barging in there hot headed with no plan?" Daniel asked. "What would be your chances of surviving?" Daniel headed for the kitchen and Jonathan followed, sighing.

"Now they have Michael too." Daniel shook his head.

"Jonathan, right now you can't afford to trust anyone," he told him. "Take a look at every one who could possibly be involved." Jonathan sat at the table and thought about what Daniel was saying.

"You're right, Dad," he finally agreed. "I'll go to the service tomorrow, but not alone." He looked up at Daniel. "I'm going to need some support." Daniel didn't hesitate to respond.

"Son, you will always have my support." There were a few minutes of silence before either one of them spoke.

"Dad, can I ask you a question?"

"Sure, son," Daniel nodded. "What's on your mind?"

"When you were growing up did you get along with Uncle Philip?" he asked. Surprised by the question, Daniel hesitated before answering.

"What makes you ask that?" he asked Jonathan.

"Just wondering about him. I'm sure he'll be there tomorrow to pay his respects," Jonathan replied. He sensed that his father was suddenly at a loss for words.

"Well," Daniel finally spoke. "We got along and we didn't get along." Jonathan gave him an interested look.

"What do you mean by that?" he questioned. Daniel began explaining.

"When we were kids we did everything together. When I was a senior in high school, your Uncle Philip was a talented sophomore and we were on the same basketball team. When your mother came along, I guess you could say she ruined our little brotherhood. I started doing things with Katherine and spending all my time with her. Philip became jealous."

"So what led to you becoming a cop and him becoming a businessman?" Jonathan asked, getting deeper into the conversation.

"After high school I went to the Air Force Academy. I stayed in the military for six years. Right after I got out your mother got pregnant with you and I joined the police force. Your uncle went to technical school up in Maine and became a very wealthy man. As you know, he does business all over the world."

"Did you two keep in touch after high school?" Jonathan asked. Daniel nodded.

"Yes, we kept in touch for a while and then he disappeared for a few years when he went to Australia. It was shortly after that when I came here so we didn't have much of a chance to keep in touch like we should have."

"You'll see him tomorrow," Jonathan grinned with excitement. His dad shook his head.

"He won't recognize me and anyway, we can't tell him about this," Daniel said.

"Why not?" Jonathan asked, disappointed.

"He wouldn't understand," Daniel explained. "He was never into fairy tales or   anything make believe. He's a very realistic person." He wanted to change the subject. "You need to grab something to eat, son. When did you eat last?" Jonathan shook his head.

"I'm not hungry right now," he said. Daniel walked over to the door leading to the patio and gazed out.

"You know, when you were a child I had a feeling that there was something different about you. Every now and then things would happen that could never be explained." Jonathan looked at his father, anxious to hear stories of his childhood that he'd never heard before. Daniel continued. "I remember one time when I took you fishing. A water moccasin bit you and before I could react you grabbed it and pulled it off of your hand. You never even cried. You crushed its head with your shoe and went on fishing. That snake never stood a chance against you." Jonathan was amazed at hearing this.

"Did Mom ever know these things?" he asked, clearing his throat.

"No Jonathan, she didn't. I knew it would be too much for her so I never told her. There were a lot of things happening that were unexplainable." He came to the table and sat down.

"Tell me something else Dad, if you can. Ever since I've been in school, kids have picked on me because I'm small. But I would all of a sudden get a burst of energy. I never knew what happened because I would always black out." Daniel began to tell the story of another incident, but started to chuckle at the thought of it. "What's so funny?" Jonathan asked.

"One time you were completely naked and jumped out of your bedroom window head first. Your mother was screaming, she just knew you had broken your neck. There's no way you should have survived that jump from the second floor! When we got outside there you were, standing up smiling at us. I knew there was something about you, but never could explain it." Daniel laughed again at the memory of that day.

"How old was I when I was doing all of these things?" Jonathan asked. Daniel gave it some thought before he replied.

"Let's see," he said. "The window stunt was when you were three and the snake encounter would have been when you were four. And believe me, son, there is a lot more to you than you know." Daniel got up from the table and headed out of the room. He could sense that Jonathan could spend all day asking questions. He turned to his son and said, "Jonathan, find something to do to occupy your mind. Tomorrow is a big day and it's not going to be easy." He went to his room and shut the door. Jonathan went into the living room and sat on the couch. He thought about the stories his father had told him, and wondered what other stories he had yet to hear. His thoughts quickly turned to Reagan. He thought back on all the time they had spent together and all the fun times they had. It wasn't long before his thoughts came to her kidnapping. This made the anger well up inside him again. For a moment he thought of going to where his house once stood. But wisdom took over as he remembered everything Daniel had said and realized he was right. Beating his fist on his knee, he vowed to himself that he would save his friends and avenge his family. Jonathan stood up and went to his room.

Chapter Twenty

Jonathan and Daniel arrived at the memorial service. Seeing the church parking lot overflowing, Jonathan parked the car a few blocks down the road. They got out of the car and walked down the street.

"Remember Jonathan, regardless of who you see in here today you have got to keep your cool." Jonathan didn't respond and Daniel continued. "There will be a lot of our family here and the place will probably erupt into chaos since most everyone will be thinking that you died too. Be ready for anyone and everyone that you meet." Jonathan's mind was focused more on rescuing his friends, especially Reagan. Most of what Daniel was saying was going in one ear and out the other. Daniel figured that's what was happening. "Are you hearing what I'm saying?" he asked his son. Jonathan nodded.

"Yes, I hear you," he replied.

"Try to keep your answers short and simple," Daniel suggested. "Dmitri may also be here today. He most likely knows who you are, but it's doubtful that he would start anything in a crowd of people." Jonathan clenched his fists.

"I really hope he does start something today, because I want his head."

They reached to door to the church. The outer doors were glass and Jonathan could see the crowd inside since the inner doors to the sanctuary were propped open. He began to sweat as he was unsure of the reaction he would get when he walked inside. As he walked into the sanctuary with Daniel right behind him, heads turned in his direction and the room filled with gasps. They were quickly followed by lots of whispers all around the room. The two men made their way up to the front as family members made room for Jonathan to sit down. Motioning to Daniel, Jonathan managed to speak. "He sits with me," he uttered. Without a word the family made more room to accommodate both of them. Sitting down Jonathan noticed the three pictures up front of his mother, sister and himself. As quickly as he saw it, a family member that he didn't recognize stood up and removed his picture. Other family members began giving him hug after hug, all of them with eyes full of tears. A sad day but a bit of hope at finding that he was alive. There were some relatives that he recognized.

His mother's sister came and hugged him and then his uncle approached him.

"Are you okay?" his uncle asked as he hugged him. Jonathan nodded.

"I'm fine," he said.

"Who is your friend?" he asked, looking at Daniel. Before Jonathan could answer, Daniel stood up and shook the man's hand.

"I'm Daniel Smith," he told him.

"I'm Jonathan's uncle. Philip Bailey." Daniel smiled.

"Nice to meet you. Jonathan has told me a lot of great things about you."

"Be sure that we get a chance to talk after the service," Philip told Daniel before taking his seat at the far end of the pew.

"I've told you a lot of great things about him?" Jonathan questioned Daniel. His father shrugged.

"I had to say something," Daniel remarked. They all sat down and the commotion that had filled the church finally came to a halt. They listened as the preacher began the service, but Jonathan couldn't help but look around. He wanted to see every face that was there. Suddenly he heard a woman's voice.

"I knew you weren't dead," the voice announced. Startled, but not wanting to draw attention to himself, he slowly looked behind him, back and forth. This caught Daniel's attention.

"What's the matter?" Daniel asked, and he began to look also, although unsure of what he was looking for. Jonathan quietly explained what he had just heard. They continued to look around. The voice spoke once again.

"Look to your left on the third row from the end." Jonathan looked and was surprised to see the psychic. He quickly turned around and faced the front.

"What are you doing here Anita?" he whispered. He was amazed that they could communicate from such a distance.

"To be honest Jonathan, I came to see you," she answered. "I know all about you and your magical powers," she went on to say. "I see you've gotten used to them."

"A lot has happened since that night," he told her. She nodded slightly, even though he couldn't see her.

"I know," she said. "I've been hiding ever since that night. I knew someone would come looking for me. I hid in a secret room in the attic. They tore the place up looking for me. I've spent the last four days keeping out of sight."

"How do you know so much about me?" Jonathan asked.

"The man sitting beside you that you came with. That's how I know so much about you. I know he's your father." Jonathan looked at Daniel and gave him a jab with his elbow. When he looked up Jonathan glanced back at Anita and Daniel looked at her and smiled.

"Why is it that you can talk to me telepathically but not him?" Jonathan queried.

"That's because of who you are," she told him. "Your mental abilities are far greater that you realize. Telepathy will come to you in time, as your powers increase."

"Anita, why hasn't my father told me all this?"

"Because he only understands the physical and magical parts of who you are", she further explained. "The mental part is my area of expertise. I can tell you this, Jonathan. Your mental powers will be far greater than the other two." Daniel interrupted them.

"Ask her if she's coming back to the mansion after the service," he said.

"Tell him yes. I will go with you," Anita answered. Jonathan turned to tell his father what she had said and then stopped himself before whipping around to look at her.

"Wait a minute," he exclaimed. "How can you know what he's saying if he doesn't have psychic abilities?" Anita held back a laugh.

"I have the ability to read minds, all minds. However, I can only communicate with those with the same ability. Just because your father can't read mine doesn't hinder my reading his."

"I'd like to listen to the service," he told her. But can I ask you one more question? We all know you're in danger, so would you please come stay with us at the mansion?" Jonathan didn't understand her hesitation until she went on to explain.

"We all used to be a team. Your father, Reagan and myself. But my sister and I didn't always see eye to eye." Jonathan had to remind himself not to react openly.

"You and Reagan are sisters?" he asked, not sure what to think.

"Yes," came her reply. "She is my younger sister. I am ten years older than her." Sensing his thoughts, she did the math for him. "I am forty eight years old."

"Please come stay with us so you'll be safe. We'll talk more after the services."

"Wait, what is it you're trying not to tell me? Either tell me or I can pry deeper into your thoughts to find out," she told him.

"It's Reagan. She was abducted by Dmitri yesterday," Jonathan confessed. He could tell that Anita was starting to cry. "You have my word Anita that I will find her and bring her back to us safely." His heart went out to her as he could see how much she loved Reagan.

"My sister always loved you, Jonathan", she told him. "And I can certainly see why. Yes, I will come to the mansion and stay with you." With a sigh of relief Jonathan turned back to face front and listen to the service. Getting back into the moment and remembering why they were all gathered, he became aware that everyone was crying. His own tears began to trickle down his face. His mind went back to that night when he ran into the house and found his family. His tears started to flow harder. Daniel noticed and put his arm around his son. As he did, he noticed out of the corner of his eye that Philip was watching them.

"It's okay son," he whispered to Jonathan. "That's right, let it all out." He tightened his embrace as he dealt with his own emotions. Leaving his family was hard, but losing them this time was definitely permanent. Jonathan reached into the inside pocket of his jacket and removed a handkerchief. He whispered to Daniel.

"Whenever I find Dmitri, wherever and whoever he is, I promise you he's a dead man." The choir began singing Amazing Grace. When they finished the preacher asked the congregation if there was anyone present who would like to say a few words to pay their respects to the Bailey family. Slowly, Jonathan stood up and made his way to the pulpit. It was a few moments before he could compose himself enough to be able to speak. He started out talking about losing his father at a young age. He thanked his uncle for being there for the family after their loss. The rest of the memories he spoke of were those of his mother and sister. He noticed that even Uncle Philip was crying. It was hard to watch the hurt and anguish in his uncle's eyes. He had never seen him upset about anything. Jonathan then looked at Daniel who gave him a thumbs up while wiping his own tears with a handkerchief. When he was finished speaking Jonathan stepped back from the podium and reflected for a few moments before returning to his seat. On his way from the pulpit he was hugged and comforted by many family members. Aunts, uncles, and numerous cousins. Uncle Philip was the last one to hug him.

"I'm always here for you, Johnny. Whenever you need me," he reassured him. They all sat down for the benediction.

Chapter Twenty One

As they arrived at the mansion Daniel and Anita went inside and Jonathan stayed outside on the porch.

"How have you been?" Daniel asked Anita. "You didn't say much on the way here." Anita thought for a few moments before replying.

"I'm okay I guess. Now that my sister is in the hands of lunatics, this will change my plans."

"What do you mean?" Daniel asked. He walked to the refrigerator and got them both something to drink.

"Thank you," she said, taking the drink. "When all of this was over I was planning on moving away from here and going to New York." She looked around as she followed Daniel into the living room to sit down. "I see the place hasn't changed," she remarked. After a brief silence she told Daniel,

"You've done a remarkable job with Jonathan. When did you tell him you were his father?"

"Just a few days ago," was his reply. "Look Anita, I'm not going to mince words," he said, his tone getting more serious. "We need you back on the team. According to the scrolls, there is something bad headed our way. A threat far worse than we could have imagined." She didn't answer right away. Daniel knew what she was thinking and had an idea what she was going to say. When she did finally speak it was almost in a whisper.

"You should know why I don't want to come back," she told him. Daniel knew that she was right and when he didn't respond she repeated herself, but this time it was louder. Daniel hung his head in disgust. "Look at me, Daniel," she demanded. "I never could get you to forget about your wife. That's why I left and don't tell me that surprises you!" Daniel turned to face her.

"Anita, you're going to have to put any feelings you still have aside. Reagan's been abducted and we need to concentrate on getting her back," he told her. Her eyes began to fill with tears. She tried wiping them away.

"I know she's missing," she retorted. "You have Jonathan. My only family has been taken from me." Her tears flowed more rapidly. "I gave my life to this place and what did

I get? A broken heart! I waited patiently with you and Reagan as we watched Jonathan grow up. I tried getting close to you, but you kept pushing me away." Daniel shook his head.

"I never said I didn't love you," he told her.

"Then what was it?" she asked.

"I just felt out of line if I started anything with you or even let anything happen between us," he explained.

"No, that wasn't it and you know it!" she yelled. She grew more aggravated with Daniel as she stood up and paced the floor. "It was your wife and the fact that you just couldn't let go of her."

"Anita, you have no idea how difficult it was for me. Katherine had nothing to do with my feelings for you. I was thinking of my son. I knew someday I would get him back and have to bring him into the life I now had."

"Leave Jonathan out of this, Daniel," she argued, pointing her finger at him. You know this was about Katherine the whole time. You couldn't let go of her, so don't try and lay this on your son."

"Anita please," Daniel started. "Put your feelings aside and think. Right now we need to stay focused on what's going on and what we have to do. Jonathan is in danger with Dmitri and the black dragon on the loose. We can't let our feelings or dreams get in the way. The mission has to be our main concern. If Dmitri does find the golden box and destroys it, Jonathan won't stand a chance, not even with Dexter's help." Daniel's tone turned to hopeful speculation. "Anita, I've seen something in Jonathan. It's too early to tell and I can't explain. Something none of us ever thought was possible."

"What are you talking about?" she asked. She was leaning against the cabinet and Daniel walked in front of her and looked directly at her.

"That day that we were in the cave," he began. "As Jonathan was retrieving the swords. I could see the golden glow that I knew to be Dexter. But there was something else, a white energy was in the center of the golden one." Anita forgot her anger and looked him in the eye.

"Are you telling me that Jonathan could be…?" Daniel interrupted her.

"I don't know. Like I said, it's far too early to tell. Regardless, we have to focus on Dmitri right now. If Jonathan can defeat him, then we will see whether or not my suspicions are true." Anita thought about what Daniel was hinting at.

"If you are correct," she said, "then that would explain why Dexter came to Jonathan. And in the event that Dmitri is destroyed, your son would have control over both of the dragons." Daniel shook his head.

"No, he would control all three of them," he corrected her. Her jaw dropped.

"Do you mean there are three dragons?" she asked. He nodded.

"According to the scrolls, yes, there are three," was his reply.

Jonathan walked through the door and Daniel stepped back. He didn't want him to see him standing so close to Anita. This was not a good time for him to find out that they had feelings for each other. Daniel motioned to Anita to change the subject as well.

"Dad, do you remember that card I found at the house that night and I gave you?" Jonathan asked.

"Yes, son. I do," Daniel replied.

"I was in the car just now going over some stuff on the computer. The card says Bailey Corp. What do you think that means?" Jonathan queried. Daniel hesitated.

"Jonathan, with so much going on right now, I really can't answer that question," his father said. Jonathan stared off into the distance momentarily before asking his next question.

"Do you think it's possible that Uncle Philip is involved in all of this?" he asked. Daniel shrugged his shoulders.

"I really don't know what to tell you, son. There are so many people connected to you, even in small ways that are involved in this. We just have to be cautious and aware of everyone around us." Jonathan looked at Anita and then back at his dad.

"How come you've never mentioned Anita before? Seems like you would have told me about her," Jonathan wondered. Anita turned to Daniel and put her hands on her hips.

"Yeah, Daniel," she started. "Why haven't you even mentioned me to Jonathan?" Daniel shook his head.

"That's not important right now." Looking to Anita he continued, "Do you think you can get a sense of something from Reagan?" After concentrating for a few minutes while the guys stood and watched, she nodded her head and smiled at them.

"I think she's okay, but I don't know where she is." Jonathan jumped into action.

"That's okay. We know where she is. And I'm going to bring her back to the mansion," he announced. He walked through the kitchen taking the back way through the classroom into the weapons room. Daniel and Anita followed him. They watched as he grabbed a full body suit and threw it over his shoulder.

"Aren't you going to take any weapons?" he asked. Jonathan shook his head.   He stood silently for a moment and took a deep breath.

"If I took any guns that would give them a break. It would be too easy on them," he replied. Daniel walked up to Jonathan and looked at the necklace. It was flashing, indicating that the time was drawing near. "It's almost time, isn't it?" Jonathan asked.   "We don't have time to wait." Agreeing with his son Daniel nodded.

"I know. You're going to have to engage in this battle with Dexter still being dormant. The world is depending on you. Tonight's the night. The world will either fall or be saved. Just trust in everything you've learned. Remember, son, whatever happens I love you and am very proud of you." They hugged each other tight.

"I love you too dad." The three of them left the room and went into the kitchen.   The two adults stayed there while Jonathan ran upstairs to change. As soon as Daniel was sure that he was out of ear shot he spoke.

"I will tell him about you when all of this is over. I admit that you were right about me not letting go of Katherine when you and I met," he said. He walked over and stood in front of her and they looked into each other's eyes. "The truth is, I let go of her long before that." Tears slowly trickled down

Anita's cheek. As she reached up to wipe them away, Daniel stopped her. He then reached up and slowly wiped her tears away. "We have a lot of work to do when all of this is over. For one thing Reagan is going to need you. She never was the same again after you left four years ago," he told her.   Jonathan came downstairs and joined them. As soon as he entered the room, Daniel quickly left and went to his own room. Jonathan gave Anita a bewildered look. He wondered what was going on. Anita shook her head and threw her hands up in the air. She had no clue either. Just as quickly as he'd left, Daniel reappeared and handed a small brown velvet bag to Jonathan.

"What is this?" Jonathan asked. He untied the drawstring to find a handful of reddish orange marbles. He still had no idea and looked at his father with a puzzled look on his brow.

"They're sleeping beads," Daniel explained. "Once they leave the bag, they emit an invisible vapor that puts people to sleep. I thought they might come in handy."   Jonathan tucked the bag into a pocket on the left leg of his uniform. Gearing up, he slowly made his way to the door leading to the garage. Reaching for the doorknob, he stopped and without turning around he smiled and said,

"I know you two have a history together. So dad, give her a chance." He opened the door and walked towards the car.

"How did you know?" Daniel asked him. Still smiling, Jonathan looked over his shoulder so that he could see their faces. He pointed to his ear.

"I heard the whole conversation from upstairs. So, like I said. Give her a chance.   We both know that Mom would have wanted you to move on." Daniel was astonished at not only having his son's approval so early after losing his family, but also at seeing that he was starting to have telepathic abilities. The more powers he had, the better it would be for him. He looked at Anita and extended his hand in her direction. She looked at it briefly, then grabbed it and smiled. "Dad I'm going to need you at the computer for extra support. And Anita, welcome home." With that Jonathan got in the car. Before driving off he reached in the glove compartment and removed Reagan's cell phone. He went through the pictures they had taken with Caroline that first day that he had met Reagan. Laying the phone on his lap, he drove off.

Chapter Twenty Two

Jonathan arrived at his destination with Daniel following the radar on the computer back at the mansion. He had done the whole trip in stealth mode so as to not be detected.

"Dad, can you find me a way in?" he asked Daniel, using the onboard intercom.

"Yes, just give me a second and I'll have it for you," came Daniel's reply. That few seconds of waiting made Jonathan antsy. He was more than anxious to get in there and take care of business. "Looks like the best way in with the Badger is through the back yard," Daniel instructed him. Jonathan drove the Lion through the rubble and around to the back of the house. Once there he transformed the car into the Badger enabling him to go underground. He began moving everything in his way; grass, rocks, etc. "You're almost there, son," Daniel told him. "Keep going straight, according to the radar you'll be coming in from the back of the place. Be very careful as we don't know what you'll find once you break through the ground."

"How much further?" Jonathan asked.

"About a quarter of a mile," Daniel replied. As he continued his descent beneath what used to be his house, Jonathan's eyes scanned every inch of the dirt in front of him. He was ready for anything. All he wanted right now was to kill Dmitri and rescue Reagan. "Dad, have you wondered how long this hideout has been here? I mean, somebody didn't just decide to put this here yesterday."

"I know what you're saying," Daniel agreed. "How in the world did they get all the materials and such down there without anybody seeing anything?" When Jonathan arrived at the enormous fortress, the Badger tore right through the wall. The commotion it caused was unavoidable and he found about twenty men waiting for him in the room. Jonathan wasn't ready to fight. He pulled out the marbles and tossed them out of the window. They rolled across the floor and before any of the men could react they were all asleep. As he got out of the car Jonathan put a tiny transmitter in his ear so he could keep in constant contact with Daniel. He cautiously went through the first door, peeking out before continuing on. "Okay now," his father said. "Keep going north and I believe you'll find Michael and the others." Jonathan didn't speak any more than he had to, so as not to be heard by Dmitri or any of his henchmen. He was in a hallway that seemed to have at least a dozen doors. He did as instructed and proceeded north. "The next door you come to will be a bit bigger room," Daniel told him. "The next room after that should be where you find Michael.

"Thanks," Jonathan whispered. Coming to the next door he stopped and put his ear to the door. He could hear a few men talking. Taking a deep breath he knocked on the door and waited for someone to answer it. When one of them finally did, Jonathan kicked him in the chest sending him into the air. Getting a quick glance he saw that he was in what looked like some sort of warehouse. He tried to get a quick headcount to see what he was up against. He counted eleven men just as they began charging him two at a time, then three at a time. "Smoke screen," he yelled and the place filled with smoke. There was a panic among the men as they lost control of the situation. "Which one of you killed my mother and sister?" he demanded, but nobody offered a confession. Not wanting to waste any time, Jonathan jumped sixteen feet into the air and caught one of the rafters and swung himself safely to the door on the other side of the room. He landed right in front of the door. Not your ordinary door, this was the size of a garage door. "Dad, is this where Michael's watch is transmitting from?" he asked.

"Yes," Daniel answered. "It's coming from right in front of you." Jonathan looked at the door before calling upon his swords. In the blink of an eye they appeared and he sliced through the door like it was paper. As the door collapsed to the floor and he stepped through Jonathan noticed at least a hundred men waiting for him, all with guns. Jonathan was amazed at how large this place was. It seemed to go forever.

"Any of you want to tell me who killed my family?" he yelled, as he looked around the room.

"I did," said Jason. He stepped forward and motioned for the remaining men to step back. As the two men glared at each other, Jonathan's face filled with hatred.

"I'm talking to a dead man," Jonathan said. Figuring he was stronger than Jonathan and would catch him off guard, Jason charged him. However, Jason quickly found himself to be no match for the younger man. Faster than the eye could see, Jonathan ducked and came back at Jason with a stabbing blow to the abdomen, knocking him to his knees. Jason couldn't breathe. There was a collective gasp from the crowd of men. They had never seen anyone get the better of Jason. Falling forward on his hands, Jason was fighting to get just one breath. With a swift kick Jonathan sent his enemy hurling in the air about twenty feet. As he came down he was met with a punch from Jonathan with both hands clasped together. It was such a vicious blow to the back that it broke Jason's spine. Although

Jonathan knew Jason was done, the anger was still there and with a final show of strength, he lifted the broken man above his head with one arm and slammed him down to the floor. Jonathan suddenly heard applause coming from somewhere above him. As he looked upwards, Jonathan's eyes grew wide. "You're Dmitri?" he demanded with surprise.

"Yes, I am," was the reply.

"Why, Uncle Philip?" he asked. Thinking nothing else could surprise him, this threw Jonathan for a loop. He watched as Philip came down some stairs carrying the golden box. Only having heard of the golden box, Jonathan was in awe of actually seeing it. "You killed your sister in law and niece," Jonathan reminded him in disbelief. Dmitri nodded.

"That's what had to be done to find this," he replied, holding up the golden box. Jonathan was hurt that there was no remorse whatsoever. It had been hard on him losing his family, but to find out it was at the hands of another family member, and one he totally trusted all his life, was almost too much to swallow. Dmitri continued. "Plus there is all this uranium underneath your parent's old house." Jonathan was trying to take this all in and with every thought he hurt more and more.

"So you killed them for uranium on your part, and the golden dragon of supremacy for Dmitri's part."

"Exactly," Dmitri smiled and nodded. He was reveling in having the upper hand. As this began to sink in, Jonathan had to fight back tears. He refused to let his emotions get the best of him. After all, he hadn't lost to Dmitri yet. Dmitri went on to explain, or better yet, to brag. "I know you've probably wondered how I got all this built underground without anyone noticing. Remember that I'm a wizard. I hypnotized people so they wouldn't pay attention to anything that was happening around here. It was built years ago. Your father was getting to close to me so that's why he was disposed of." Jonathan shot him a look of anger.

"So you're responsible for that too?" he exclaimed. He could see that Philip was proud of every move he had made. He regretted nothing. This made every ounce of hurt inside Jonathan be replaced by two ounces of hatred. Hatred towards his uncle.

"That wasn't the only reason I killed your father," Dmitri admitted. "Our blood line is of great power. Your father and I were the only males. Then you were born." When Jonathan didn't think he could hate Philip any more than he already did, Philip would say something else. Every word was pouring the anger and hatred into his nephew. Jonathan fought back his feelings, he wasn't quite ready to engage Dmitri in battle. Dmitri held up the golden box. "This is what this entire mission was about," he announced. With your uncle dealing in uranium, that just made everything fall into place. Don't forget his greed, couldn't have worked so well without that." Jonathan continued to stare daggers at his enemy.

"My father isn't the one that Dexter came to. It was me," he confided.

"I know that now, but the fact remains that he is the only one who can open the golden box and release the dragon, and he has finally been revived." Dimitri continued to explain. "I couldn't open the box because of my impure heart. It was deemed that my heart was too filled with negativity. When our father created the dragons, they were created for each other, but I wanted more. That's why I killed our father and strangled my brother in his sleep. However his spirit didn't die because..." Jonathan quickly interrupted him.

"I know that the only way a wizard can die is at the hands of another wizard. Tell me something I don't know," he retorted sarcastically. "So you killed my father because you expected that he would be the one chosen by Dexter. Well, the laugh's on you because Dexter's spirit is here, whether or not he is revived. And I will defeat you." All of Dmitri's men continued to stand and watch. Dmitri turned to look at them over his shoulder.

"Don't any of you get involved in this battle," he commanded them. "Doing away with this punk once and for all will be my pleasure. All mine." The men formed a circle around Dmitri and Jonathan. Dmitri looked down at Jason and shook his head. "I see what you can do. You took down my top man." He extended his hand over Jason and in the blink of an eye Jason's body disintegrated. Jonathan was filled with disgust at seeing someone be that cold hearted. "That's what happens when you fail," said Dmitri. He handed the golden box to one of his henchmen and stood in a direct line facing Jonathan. Knowing the battle was at hand, Jonathan took a stance to prepare for whatever was to come his way. Dmitri charged at him, but with such speed that Jonathan never saw a thing. Coming past him, Dmitri slapped him in the chest, knocking him to his butt and sliding across the floor. Jonathan quickly jumped to his feet and was aware that the evil one was standing behind him. Anticipating the next move Jonathan was able to dodge Dmitri's next swing. Bending down to his knees as the swing came, Jonathan was able to send a piercing blow to his opponent's abdomen. He then came up under Dmitri with a sharp undercut to the chin, and moved away to put distance between Dmitri and himself. Jonathan then picked himself up off the floor rubbing his face. "That was good," Dmitri admitted to his nephew. "You move fast." Jonathan braced himself. He knew this was far from being over. They ran at each other simultaneously as Jonathan yelled.

"Smoke screen!" And smoke began filling the area directly around them. The circle the men had formed was on the outside of the smoke. They could only stand and wonder what was happening inside. They could hear the commotion, but that was it. The battle raged between the two Bailey men. Dmitri hit Jonathan across the face with such force that it sent him flying out of the smoke screen and up against a wall. He didn't hesitate to charge back in and serve his uncle a painful blow to the ribcage, knocking the air out of him. This time it was Dmitri's turn to go flying out of the smoke screen. His men didn't know what to make out of what they were seeing. Dmitri was shocked to see how strong Jonathan was even without Dexter or the golden dragon. The smoke cleared as the elder man walked back into the circle and Jonathan stood up.

"I'm tired of playing around with you," Dimitri yelled. His eyes turned black and the necklace that hung from his neck exploded. He began to hum and the hum slowly turned into a deep growl. At the same time black smoke filled the room and suddenly formed the dragon of treachery. The dragon roared as Dmitri laughed loudly. The dragon then disappeared inside Dmitri's body. Jonathan knew what this meant, knew the power that this instantly gave his uncle.

He thought to himself, "Now what am I supposed to do?" Before he could come up with any ideas, the black dragon disappeared from sight. Panic began to take hold as he felt himself losing control of the situation. He looked from side to side trying to see anything. He was suddenly hit from behind and went flying forward. That was quickly followed by a kick from the front to the abdomen that sent him flying backwards. Jonathan once again went sliding across the floor, this time gasping for air. He laid there panting as he watched the dragon come towards him. With his left hand Dmitri raised Jonathan up above him, holding only the young man's neck. His right hand lit up and he gave Jonathan a blast to the chest. This sent him flying into some of the men still forming a circle, and they all collapsed to the floor. Jonathan managed to get to his feet, although in a daze. He was realizing he was in over his head, but Jonathan refused to give up. He continued to try and catch his breath. Dimitri once again walked calmly towards Jonathan, laughing as he did.

"You should have given up by now," Dmitri told him. As he got closer to him, Jonathan took a wild swing. Not being able to move with the great speed he once had, Dmitri caught his arm in mid swing and began punching Jonathan with both fists. Dmitri's speed was so great that nobody in the room could see his hands move. They could only see Jonathan's body react. "Black electric web," Dmitri yelled. A huge web came out from the side of his hip and pinned Jonathan to the wall. He then ordered his men to open a fiery pit they had covered and hidden. The pit was made as they were digging to find the golden box. Instead of filling the whole back up with dirt, Dmitri had decided to use it for torture. Giving Jonathan an evil grin he commanded his men, "Bring out his friends, one at a time." The first one they brought out was Michael. Charles and Reagan were led out behind him. Jonathan's vision was blurry at first, but was starting to clear up. Dmitri walked over to the man he had handed the golden box to and took it from him. The first person that Jonathan's eyes focused on was Reagan. He couldn't just lay there while Dmitri killed her. He knew what his uncle had planned for his friends. As he violently struggled to get free, he screamed as the web sent electrical shocks through his body. They were just strong enough to cause pain. "Each time you move you'll get a big shock. A smart man would know to be still, Dmitri told him laughing. Michael, Charles, and Reagan stood helpless as they watched Jonathan writhe in pain. Reagan began to cry. Jonathan's vision went blurry again and all he could think about was how he had failed his family. Dmitri pointed his finger at the pit and it filled with hot lava. The heat coming from the lava was so great that the whole room felt like a sauna. Dmitri got Jonathan's attention real quick. "Before your friends go into the pit, this box will go in first," he said. He held it up so Jonathan could get a good look at it. As he saw the golden shine Dmitri pitched it into the lava. He felt broken as it disappeared from sight. "Your quest has come to an end, Jonathan," Dmitri bragged. He walked over to Michael and motioned to his nephew. "Do you have anything to say to your friend before you die?" he asked him. Dmitri grabbed the young bully by the back of the neck.

"Jonathan I'm sorry for all the mean things I've done to you since we were kids. I wish I could take it all back. Please forgive me," he pleaded. He dropped his head. Dmitri lifted him off the ground.

"Nooooooooo!" Jonathan screamed. "Dmitri, don't do this!" he begged. Ignoring his nephew, Michael was thrown into the pit. His screams were only heard for a couple of seconds. "No, Michael," he whispered. Dmitri then walked up to Charles and grabbed him behind the neck. "Stop this madness, Uncle Philip," Jonathan cried.

"Your Uncle Philip died a long time ago when he submitted himself to me," Dmitri explained. "He did all of this, turned his back on his family, all for more power. Charles, do you have anything to say to your best friend?" Charles starting crying.

"Man, my dad was in way over his head. That's the reason I'm here, but I should have told you when I found out. I'm sorry." Dmitri picked him up and dangled him for Jonathan to see. He held him longer than he had Michael.

"Don't do it, Dmitri," Jonathan pleaded. "Charles hasn't done anything. He doesn't deserve this. None of them do. This is all about the golden box and you've already destroyed that. Please let him go!" Jonathan looked into his friends' eyes as he watched him be thrown into the lava. Just as

Michael had, he only screamed for a moment. "Charles, NOOOOO!" he screamed as loud as he could. This was far more than Jonathan had ever imagined could happen. As tears poured down his face, the room seemed to grow quiet and Jonathan reflected on his family and his friends. He kept his eyes closed and cried. Suddenly he saw another pair of eyes open while his were still closed. He began to yell, as he knew what this meant. He knew what was happening. The moment had come. Dexter was revived. His scream was so loud it probably could have been heard all over the planet. Jonathan opened his eyes and watched as the building began to shake and all of Dmitri's men fell to the floor. Dmitri stood in amazement, but still confident in himself. He had destroyed the golden box. Jonathan broke free from the web, throwing it to the floor. Still screaming he got to his feet and the scream became that of two people. Dexter had joined him. It was only a few seconds before the necklace shattered and golden smoke emerged from the lava and filled the room. It gathered behind Jonathan and formed the dragon of supremacy. The dragon let out a roar so fierce that it could be heard throughout the universe. Dmitri suddenly lost his confidence and became frightened. He extended his hand and sent a blast of energy hurling at the dragon. He was soon to realize he was no match for the dragon as he watched his energy blast disintegrate in midair. The golden dragon entered Jonathan's body. The screaming stopped and the dragon looked down at Dmitri. Finally Dexter spoke.

"I see things haven't changed, dear brother," he said.

"I should have killed you long ago," Dmitri shot back. Terrified and panicked, he ordered his men to attack. The men all charged at Jonathan together. The dragon raised its hands as the men came at him. Just as they reached him, the dragon dropped his hands and they men were instantly frozen in a golden fluid.

"You should know that these mere mortals can't stand up to us," Dexter said. He clapped his hand and the frozen concoction shattered like glass, along with everyone that was inside. "Jonathan, are you ready?" he asked.

"You bet," came Jonathan's reply. Dmitri wasn't sure what to expect. It was odd the way he was staring at the dragon and hearing both voices talking to each other from within. "Duo technique," they shouted simultaneously. Dexter and Jonathan separated, but Dexter took on the appearance of Jonathan except with longer hair. He stood in a golden robe with long black hair. He nodded towards Reagan. "Go get your girl and I'll take care of him." He turned his gaze on Dmitri. Hearing what was said and knowing he was done for, Dmitri sent a blast at Reagan. He knew he was about to lose, but the evil just couldn't give up.

237 | The Teaching

"No!" Jonathan shouted. Reading Dexter's mind he knew to snap his fingers at the same time as Dexter. The blast of energy that Dmitri sent out began losing speed and moved almost at a snail's pace. This gave Jonathan time to get to Reagan and deflect the blast. Kneeling down, he picked her up. "Are you okay?" he asked her. She was so elated and relieved that she couldn't even answer Jonathan. She just held on to him tightly.

"Now it's my turn," shouted Dexter. Clasping his hands together he created a golden ball of energy. As he slowly opened his hands the ball grew in size. When he was ready, Dexter threw it at his brother. Anticipating what Dexter would do, Dmitri was able to dodge the projectile. Unfortunately for him, that took his attention away from Dexter. When he turned back around Dexter was standing right in front of him and started punching all over his body, from the face down to the abdomen. The punches were coming so rapidly that Dmitri's body was going in every direction all at once.

Jonathan pressed a button on his body suit that hailed the badger.

"Listen, Reagan", he said. He handed her a small remote. "Take this. I need you to run through that door and wait for the car. When it gets to you push the button on the remote and it will stop." She gave him a meaningful kiss and ran through the door. As Jonathan turned his attention back to the battle between the brothers, he saw Dexter kick Dmitri in the face, sending him flying back towards the lava pit. In the blink of an eye Jonathan was there and with a kick of his own sent his uncle back towards Dexter. Dmitri was able to catch himself in midair. He stopped and came slowly down to the ground. He stood right in front of Dexter, weakened from all the blows they had dealt him. Jonathan walked over and stood next to Dexter. "Uncle Philip," Jonathan began, looking at him with disgust. "Or whoever you are. This ends now. You've been plaguing my family and friends long enough. People have died needlessly because of you." Dexter and Jonathan stood shoulder to shoulder. Simultaneously they shouted.

"Neutron blast!" This blast came out of nowhere and hit Dmitri square in the chest. This brought him to his knees, and the blast continued on and carried him into the lava pit causing a huge explosion. "Shield!" they shouted, this time as they were joining back together as one.

"We're not going to make it out", Jonathan feared. From within him he heard Dexter speak.

"Now that I have been revived you can fly, my boy." Jonathan immediately left his feet and flew to meet Reagan at the car. As soon as they reached the surface the car turned into the golden eagle and they headed for the mansion.

Chapter Twenty Three

"Jonathan! Wake up, Jonathan," hollered Reagan. She began to shake him to wake him. "Did you have another nightmare? Tell me, sweetheart, what's troubling you?" Jonathan sat up and swung his feet over the edge of the bed. All the sweat pouring down his face made him feel as if he were standing under a waterfall. "What's the matter?" she asked again.

"Nothing," Jonathan replied, shaking his head. Reagan placed her hand on his back. He knew she had no intention of letting this go. "Well," he began. "Reagan, I can't really remember all of it. Just bits and pieces." He turned around and looked her in the eyes. "All I remember is that I was fighting an extremely powerful being and he was getting the best of me. Really, that's all I remember." He turned back around facing the wall, and Reagan stretched her legs out beside his and wrapped her arms around his waist.

"Baby, it's just a dream," she reassured him. Jonathan nodded his head.

"Yeah, maybe you're right." Deep down in his heart he knew this was more than just a dream. Reagan convinced him to lay back down with her. As they laid there in each other's arms, Jonathan's phone rang. "Hello?" He sat up in bed.

"Hey son. You need to get down here," Daniel told him. "I have something to show you."

"Is it important?" Jonathan asked.

"Very." Jonathan quickly jumped up, got dressed and headed downstairs to the program room. As he opened the door and went in, he noticed Daniel standing in front of an 80 inch screen, his hands clasped behind his back.

"What is it?" Jonathan asked. He came up beside his father and studied the screen.

"I don't know, but whatever it is, it's making its way towards earth at double the speed of light."

"Can you enhance it or make it bigger?" Jonathan queried. Daniel pressed a button on the remote and the image grew. "It's some kind of a ship," Daniel announced, pointing to the screen.

"The ship is from Newmania." Both men turned as they heard Maximus' voice as he came into the room.

"What are you talking about?" Jonathan asked. "And where exactly is Newmania?" Maximus stood beside the two men and they all studied the screen. Maximus explained.

"It's a planet much like earth. It's in the center of the Andromeda Galaxy and the only inhabited planet in that galaxy. The planet, however, is ruined."

"Why?" asked Daniel and Jonathan simultaneously.

"Sad really," began Maximus. "It's all due to their ruler, Xantese. He's a tyrant and has taken every living thing on the planet and dried it out. As is to be expected, that didn't help his people's way of living."

"How is it that you know so much about all of this?" Jonathan asked. Daniel crossed his arms.

"I was just going to ask the same question," he said. "How do you know all of this and yet we've never heard of this planet before?"

"It's all in the scrolls that you defeated him. Now you must prepare for this next battle if what's written in the scrolls is to ever come true."

"When is this ship supposed to get here?" Jonathan asked. "Is this tyrant on the ship? Is he alone? When is all of this supposed to take place?"

"All I know at this time is that it will take him five years to arrive here. And it is going to take more than Dexter to defeat him." Maximus continued, "Jonathan, I cannot tell you everything I know. Some things you have to find out for yourself, including who you are."

"Then I have at least five years to train and prepare," he announced as he walked out of the room. Maximus turned to look Daniel in the eyes.

"Daniel, you do know, don't you? Who he is?" Nodding his head, Daniel replied.

"Yes, I do. He is the great wizard, reincarnated. But how, Maximus?"

"I can't explain it all right now. But in time it will be revealed that there is far more to your son than meets the eye." He lowered his head. "The Newmanian king is a very powerful being. They won't be able to fight this battle on earth. Because of the power of both of them, they will have to fight somewhere like Jupiter. Jonathan has no idea of even a portion of his power and might. He will only realize and understand it as he reaches his full potential." Maximus headed towards the portal to return to the future. "Remember, Daniel…even though the scrolls say that Jonathan will win this battle, doesn't mean that's what will happen. We don't know what all will take place until it does."

"I know," Daniel said, rubbing his chin. As the portal closed, Daniel turned back to towards the screen and stared at the ship. "Whatever or whoever you are, we will be ready."

Visit www.IslandEntertainmentMedia.com for
more information on getting your book
published, or to order individual volumes.